The Raven Mockers came a-drifting to where I could see them again. Lord in heaven, how ugly those things were, with their flapping wing-skins and their stubby legs and their mask faces. They trundled a cage along the ground with them. I reckoned I could see Luke a-standing up inside it, with his arms spread out and his hands grabbed hold of the crossbars of branches, the way a man grabs onto the window bars when he's in the jail house . . .

THE OLD GODS WAKEN

MANLY WADE WELLMAN

BERKLEY BOOKS, NEW YORK

This Berkley book contains the complete
text of the original hardcover edition.

THE OLD GODS WAKEN

A Berkley Book / published by arrangement with
Doubleday & Company, Inc.

PRINTING HISTORY
Doubleday edition published 1979
Berkley edition / May 1984

ISBN: 0-425-07015-8

A BERKLEY BOOK ® TM 757,375
Berkley Books are published by The Berkley Publishing Group,
200 Madison Avenue, New York, New York 10016.
The name "BERKLEY" and the stylized "B" with design
are trademarks belonging to Berkley Publishing Corporation.
PRINTED IN THE UNITED STATES OF AMERICA

*Great perils have this beauty, that they bring
to light the fraternity of strangers.*

—Victor Hugo

I

Things started that morning in the third week in June, when Mr. Creed Forshay left out of his cabin and headed up the struggling trail on the steep side of Wolter Mountain, to check on the flow of water from the spring that fed to the pipes for his place.

It was a rare, bright day, Mr. Creed allowed to himself. Summer was a-climbing over spring here in the mountains. Mr. Creed was a middling tall, chunky-made fellow, with bushy gray hair and a square face chopped with strong lines. He was dressed more or less usual, jeans pants stuck into high laced boots and a blue hickory work shirt with a bag of roll-your-own tobacco in the pocket, and his black old umbrella hat that had cost him maybe thirty dollars some years back. He wasn't young any more, but a good sight short of being old. He was a good farmer and a good hunter and all sorts of a good man.

He tromped across the hollow where his fish pond twinkled, a-looking up to sloping, terraced fields of corn and vegetables and to an apple orchard and nice stands of pine beyond. Forshays had owned that land all the way back to the first settlement times, in or around the year the Revolutionary War was fought to its end. And it might could be that Mr. Creed Forshay and his big son Luke worked it as well as air Forshay known to history. Loving that land helped a right much. Both Mr. Creed and Luke had been away in their times. Mr. Creed served in the Navy when he was young, had been a machinist who came back able to string his own rural electrification wires and lay his pipes to carry the spring water. And Luke had gone to Shenstone College, a-working his way through Shenstone College with good history and English grades and a-playing a patch of football. But both were there at their own place that June, because they didn't much care to be air other place else on this earth.

Above and ahead of Mr. Creed jumped up Wolter Mountain, all the great big high humps and bunches of it, grown over with trees of air kind you could call for. Under his boots, the trail went a-shammocking up the steep, woodsy face, tight and narrow as a lap of cord. The mountain kept it narrow from side to side. Going up, you moved close against the face to your right, and to your left there dropped down what might could be the death of you if you set a foot out of place.

But his cleated soles knew the way, from years of it. He tramped that way toward where he was headed, taking his usual care at the narrow-rough places. He made note of vines and trees, he relished the flowers. He saw purple wake-robin, blue spiderwort, little rosy bits on the twisted-stem. Where leaf rot made it rich under a clump of hickory, yellow trout lilies; under some pines, pouchy pink moccasin flower and three-bird orchids, red and white with a white gape like the mouths of baby birds. The pale blooms were gone off the serviceberry and the dogwood, but he spied a tuft of late windflower, white with its tad of pink. The branches of a gum showed shaggy with the close bunches of witches'-broom. Folks said that grew where someone had been murdered. If witches'-broom grew air place murder had happened round Wolter Mountain, there'd be a sight of it no matter where you roamed.

A-clambering, Mr. Creed couldn't see all the way to the top of that winding, snaking trail with the steep rocks and thick-growing plants to the one side and a long, long jump down on the other. But he'd clambered it so often he could tell air turn and jog of it, and he well knew what was up above. That was where it came to a flat amongst taller heights and hikes, and there flowed the spring. The trail, as his own feet had more or less driven it out, went between the cliff and a patch of rocks to the spring. He came on up that-a-way, out from between two pines, to where he could see the flat as always. Only today there was something different.

A couple of men were there ahead of him. He knew them by sight.

They were brothers, Brummitt and Hooper Voth, and round about six weeks back they'd taken the old Gibb place. That was the mountaintop piece of foresty flat and slope that right here bordered the Forshay land.

You'd better know something about the Gibb place and the Gibb family. Those Gibbs had found their way in, like the Forshays, in that first old time of settlement. From the first they'd been a right odd lot. Even amongst mountain-dwelling people, who've got a fair gift of minding their own business, the Gibb crowd had held off from neighbors, generation after generation. The last one of them all had been old Jonathan Gibb, who'd nair married, nair farmed, who hadn't even grown him a garden. For money to live on, he'd raised hogs on the acorns and chestnuts from his trees, and he'd blockaded fair to middling good whiskey. He'd remarked, the few times he talked to somebody, that if you tried to plow a furrow on his place, the rain and thunder and lightning came down. Nor would he allow one tree on his place to be cut. Back when the timber companies worked Wolter Mountain, he'd prowled round

3

under his pine and oak woods with a shotgun, to run off air soul a-coming there with an axe.

Lately he'd died, maybe from sickness or old age, nobody knew what. He nair left chick nor child, brother nor cousin, to heir his property. But it had come up at the county seat that he'd made a written deal that the land would go after he died to the Voth brothers.

The Voths had turned out to be as standoffish as air Gibb in history. They stayed to themselves. They went to Sky Notch, the closest town, only to shop supplies and pick up mail. Mr. Creed had run into them there a couple of times, and when he'd passed them the time of day, why, they'd just nodded to him without a-passing it back. The line of the Jonathan Gibb property they'd taken ran just at the foot of a grassy slope. On that slope had long ago been laid out a sort of figure of stones. This side of the slope ran a flat patch, mostly rocks, funny-looking rocks, to the side of Mr. Creed's trail.

Just now, when Mr. Creed got there that morning, the two Voth brothers were a-busying themselves with a posthole digger and some locust stakes, a-putting in a line of posts for a fence, right up against the edge of that very trail of Mr. Creed's.

"Hidy," Mr. Creed hailed them, quiet and cool. "Do youins have any objection to telling me why you're out here today, a-fencing off a chunk of my land?"

They wheeled on their feet to look at him. It was the closest he'd stood to them so far. Brummitt Voth was tall and lean and looked maybe a little small bit elegant, with a checked vest on over his black shirt and an expensive white hat.

"Your land, sir?" he repeated to Mr. Creed, in his voice that had a sort of salt-and-pepper touch of the English accent. "Your land?" he said. "According to the records at the courthouse, it's our land."

4

"What records are them, and in what courthouse do you say they are?" Mr. Creed inquired him, still quiet about it.

"I refer to the county courthouse, in the office of the register of deeds," said Brummitt Voth. "The original grant, as kept there, describes the line between the properties as running along the separating trail."

Mr. Creed stared from one Voth to the other. "That there description harks back near about two hundred years," he told them, his voice getting deeper. "In them old days, the trail run the far side of this here stony patch youins want to take over."

He motioned with his broad hand to the patch he called his. It was maybe an acre and a half, a flat piece in that little fold of Wolter Mountain, and it looked about halfway paved with the funny-looking rocks. Some of those rocks had some way the look of faces if you looked hard; deep eyes and stubby noses and big wide mouths, the sort of face a monkey shows you.

"The official description of the grant definitely states the trail as the boundary," put in Hooper Voth, the other brother. He was as heavy-built as Mr. Creed, though not so hard-packed in the build. His face had a thin yellowy mustache, and his tongue wetted his lower lip when he talked. "In any case," he went on to say, "I can't imagine why you'd care. You don't farm this particular ground. It shouldn't be of any value to you."

He squinted his eye over that, and it was pale like his brother Brummitt's eye, at one of the rocks that had a monkey look.

"Long ago, the trail run up yonder, above this here patch." Mr. Creed pointed to show where. "I made this here new trail myself, trod it out with my own feet. I get back and forth on it to my spring, what I get my water from." Up ahead, past the Brummitts, the spring poured

5

out of a high face of rock into a scooped-out basin, to make a flow through wire netting into the plastic pipe.

"But the description of the land calls the trail the line of demarcation," said Hooper Voth again, a-hooking a meaty thumb in his broad belt. There just might could have been a gun in his pants pocket right below that point.

"No, sir," said Mr. Creed, his voice getting hot at last. "Youins got your holdings figured dead wrong, gentlemen. I'll be obliged if you just take down them posts, and do it right now while I'm here a-watching."

"The post stay where they are, Mr. Forshay," said Brummitt Voth, and he moved to stand close to his brother. The two of them ranged like that, the tall one and the meaty one, beside the tree stakes they'd already put in the ground. Mr. Creed studied them up and down, thinking whether he might could be able to handle both of them at once if they quarreled.

"I suggest that we be rational," said Brummitt Voth. "You may go to court if you wish, Mr. Forshay. And when the judge consults the original grants of these lands, you can hear him tell you that we have the rights by which we stand here."

"Devil be damned!" came out Mr. Creed at them, loud and mad. "You two should ought to take a good look at me before you try to shove me off my own ground that's been in the Forshay family since two hundred years back about. I'm a-telling you one more time, get off my place."

"We stay on our own place," said Brummitt Voth, and "Yes," said Hooper Voth, "we stay here."

"Then stay here till I get back, you two devil-damned outlander thieves," Mr. Creed hollered them. "I'm a-going now, and when you see me again I won't be alone against the two of you. My son Luke knows the law, and he

6

knows how to deal with somebody a-trying to take the law into his own hands. You wait here for us to go deeper into the matter."

When he'd said that, he swung round and headed off again, the way he'd come. As he went, he could feel the prod of their tin-colored eyes in his back, like the muzzles of pointing guns.

He slammed down that chancy trail, near about too fast for careful safety. He was so pure down mad, he never took the time to feel scared that one of the Voths might out with a gun and open up on him. Not that Mr. Creed was much of a one to get scared easy. He'd seen too much of life, in different places, to feel that a scared fellow prospers on this earth.

He got down to the lower ground and came a-hurrying along past his fish pond toward his square-logged, shake-roofed cabin.

There on the door-log sat his long tall son Luke with his banjo, and I myself was a-sitting there beside Luke. I had my silver-strung guitar. The two of us were a-working out some breaks on a duet of "Laurel Lonesome."

"I vow, Papa, you look more or less ready to bite somebody in two," said Luke, getting up. He was round about twenty-seven years old. His fair hair was long and wavy, and he was strong in his bones and muscles, but built rangy where his father was built stocky.

"This is my friend John, Papa," said Luke. "I met up with him last Saturday at that singing in Sky Notch, and I invited him to come over and stay with us a week."

II

The way I've just been a-telling, Mr. Creed was powerful mad at what had gone with the Voths, but nair in his life did he forget his manners with somebody he reckoned was worth a show of them. I'd stood up, too, and Mr. Creed shoved out his hand to me. It was as big and broad as mine, and had a good grip to it when we shook.

"I'm proud to know you, John, and right happy that Luke bid you come stay a spell," he said. "I've heard tell of you from the Obray Ramseys in Madison, and the Herrons up in the Rebel Creek neighborhood, and Preacher Frank Ricks. They allow that, since Mr. Bascom Lamar Lunsford went to his rest, you're likely to know more of the old-timey songs than air soul left on Earth."

"People are mostly kind about listening to me," I said.

He gave a glance to where I'd put down my silver-strung guitar. "Later on, when maybe I've got rid of a thing I'm a-studying to do just now, you'll up and pick and sing for us."

"I'll do that thing, sir," I promised him. "And Luke can help me out on the banjo, he relishes to learn sweet music."

"But I want to ask what made you mad, Papa," Luke put in a word. "I can't figure who in these parts would be witless enough to go foul of you."

"You got it right, son," said Mr. Creed to him. "I've been made pure down mad by them low-flung Voth brothers, up yonder at the old Gibb place on Wolter."

8

With that, he filled us both in on what had taken place with him up the trail to his spring, how the Voths had as good as vowed him they'd take that piece of rocky ground up yonder. Hearing him, I gathered that the Voths might could turn out mean.

"They didn't ask me, they told me," Mr. Creed finished up. "I'm honest to say, if they'd acted the man with me and not the damn dog—if they'd asked me nice could they have it, I just likely would have give it to them free, for neighborly good will. But the chance of that happening is gone and past. Come on, Luke, you and me's a-going back and make them haul up them stakes with their backteeth. John, if you'd excuse us for maybe an hour of time—"

"Let's have John come along with us," said Luke, with a scowl like his daddy's. "I know he acts like a more or less peaceable sort of fellow, Papa; but here and there the talk is, when somebody started something, John finished it up for him."

Mr. Creed gave me a studying look. "You're a stranger within our gates," he said after a second, "but if you'll be with us in this, maybe help us out with the knowledge I hear tell you have, I'll be pleased."

"So will I be pleased, sir," I said back to him.

Luke and I set our instruments inside the door. Mr. Creed went to his rack of guns and chose out a good old deer rifle, German by the look. Luke slid a snubby-nosed pistol into the pocket of his jeans pants. They offered me my choice of guns, but I thanked them kindly and said I'd better do without. Then all three of us headed for the trail up to the spring.

I've got to say right out, I more or less enjoyed that walk up the mountain. Sure enough, it was a trail as lean as a whip and as steep as a bear slide, but I was like the Forshays, brought up to run mountain ridges and shelves.

I did all right, though a couple of times I hung to vines or branches. "Looky yonder," I said to Mr. Creed, maybe to get him into less of a black state of mind. "Mushrooms—good eating."

"I wouldn't touch them toadstools," he said. "Air time I look at one, it's like as if I see a toad a-sitting on it."

His mood was staying black.

Luke went up ahead, and he came to the top. He gave a little low whoop, and waved to us. We caught up with him.

"I don't see those fence stakes," said Luke.

And there wasn't a single stake by the rocky patch. A-coming to the trailside to look, I saw holes where they'd been.

"Shoo," sniffed Mr. Creed, "they must have thought better of taking the law into their own hands. They pulled them stakes up when I said I'd go fetch Luke to argue about it."

Luke went on farther, to where the spring was. I stood and gave a gaze up to the stone-set figure on the slope beyond the patch the Voths had decided not to fence in after all.

It was something to see. Big stones, boulders you might say, had been fetched together to make the outline. I should reckon it would be forty feet up and down the slope and twenty from side to side, a chunky body of bunched stones and a head on top, and short legs and long arms a-hanging down. Those stones were bigger than the monkey-faced ones in the patch the quarrel had been about. Without having aught of a way to be sure, I made a guess that some stones in that figure were tons heavy. And they must have been carried long ways from yonder here and there, especially to get them in the right shapes, chunky ones to lay close together for the body part, lean ones end to end for arms and legs.

"Just what's it meant to be, Mr. Creed?" I inquired him.

"Some sort of man shape, I reckon," he said.

"A right peculiar man shape," I had to say back. "Look how it humps in the shoulders, and the head seems like as if it snouts out. And those arms and legs aren't rightly man arms and legs. It could stand up and put its hands to the ground, like what they call an orangutan."

"Rangatang," he tried to repeat after me. "Nobody knows much about it, away off from everywhere and older than the oldest. My first folks here allowed the Indians told them it was here before the Indians remembered. Only, who'd be here to shape it up before the Indians? They were the first people here, I done heard science men say."

"I've been told a couple of tales about an older kind of folks than the Indians," I said, looking at the rocks.

"That fits the thing the Indians said, what time they'd talk to a white settler," said Mr. Creed, nodding his head. "Whatever built it, it must have been something besides just the foxes and frogs round about here."

"I know an Indian over Sky Notch way," I said. "Reuben Manco. He might could have something to say about it. Those are sure enough big old rocks."

"Some of them must be six or eight feet long, they'd weigh like a house, near about," he said, spitting on the ground. "It wonders you how folks could get them dragged round up here into the shape of that there thing. They didn't have no machines back then—not even horses, I've heard say."

He looked brighter now.

"Anyway," he said, really happy, "them Voth brothers has got themselfs off my land and their stakes with them. Didn't wait to argue no more."

"They might could have taken second thoughts and seen the right of it was on your side," I made offer. "What if they turned out to be good neighbors after all, no hard feelings?"

"That'd be fine," said Mr. Creed. "I don't love trouble no more than the next fellow."

Luke hailed us from up at the spring. We walked that-a-way to see what it was up to.

It was a right good spring, it looked like as if it had been there for long years. It had washed through the gray rock to make a sort of little cave for itself, coming down, I judged, from the heights of Wolter Mountain behind and over it. There was a good basin for the water to gather into, big as a kitchen sink. The Forshays had begun their line of plastic pipe there, mooring it right to the rock with a couple of iron bolts wedged into cracks. A funnel fetched the water in, and across that was wired an old screen sieve to keep out silt and gravel. The water in the basin looked as crystal clear as ever I saw.

"Is it sweet water?" I inquired Luke.

"Don't drink of it right now," he warned me off. "Look here what was hanging on it."

He held it out. I saw a chain like what's used for a locket, and from it hung a round piece of yellow metal—I wondered, could it be gold?—about as wide across as an old-timey pocket watch. On it was cut a cross, with some kind of chisel, rough but deep driven. Around that, inside the rim, had been chipped a circle, so that the arms of the cross, up and down and left and right, touched to it.

"I vow, that couldn't be too bad a charm to put on us," allowed Mr. Creed, bending to look. "It's got a cross to it, like a church house."

"But the cross is inside a circle," I pointed out to him. "I've happened one time to read in a book about old England, where it said crosses in circles were heathen charms there before they ever had churches."

"Them Voths has a dialect kindly like Englishmen," said Mr. Creed. "I thought that when them and me was a-talking just now."

I took a handkerchief from the pocket of my old pants and spread it out. Luke put the thing into it and I wrapped it up and stowed it away. While I was a-doing that, Luke craned his neck up the slope beyond the field where the rock picture lay.

"Who's that up yonder?" he flung out.

A man stood there, just at the humpy shoulder of the stone figure. From where we were at the spring, he was too far away for us to say if he was big or little, old or young. He had a black look to him all over, like somebody coated in tar. We looked at him, and I reckon he looked at us.

"What does he want?" Luke said.

"Whatever he wants, it's Voth property up on that rise," said Mr. Creed. "Since they turned out nice enough to leave out of my land, I don't figure I'll go on theirs."

"He's gone, anyway," I said.

And he was, just like that, just like being blinked out of sight.

"Where'd he get to?" asked Luke. "I didn't see him leave."

"He did go sudden-like," said Mr. Creed. "Gentlemen, what you say we go home and think about noon dinner? This here running over the mountain has got me hungry."

Down trail we headed again. I walked last, not knowing the way as surely as Mr. Creed or Luke. Once I had a notion that somebody else was along behind, and turned to see who. But if there'd been anybody there, he bobbed from sight like a lamp going out. I started to mention this out loud, but I kept it till later.

Back to the cabin, and in we went. Luke waved us away from the sink.

"Don't take any water for a minute," he warned us. "I want to test it."

Mr. Creed grinned at him. "I take it you don't trust them Voths."

"Let's just be sure. Come into my room, John."

He had one back bedroom, his father had the other. In there against a wall, Luke had built a bench. He had chemistry stuff—test tubes, some bottles of stuff, a couple of burners and so on. I watched while he did his testing.

"Nobody's put in any poison so far," he said at last.

"No poison," I nodded. "Just this cross in the circle. Luke, did you think somebody followed us down trail?"

"I thought that, but I couldn't make out anybody. I wonder if it was one of the Voths. If it was, they saw that we came up there with guns. I hope we're through having trouble with them."

"I hope that same thing," I said.

While Luke had tested the water, Mr. Creed had been a-cooking. He'd made some corn dodgers in a skillet and coffee in a pot, and he sliced up some good cold ham. Before Luke sat down at the table, he filled a couple of pails and three jugs with water from the tap and stowed them under the old iron sink. "That will be enough for us until tomorrow morning," he said. "I'll give the water another test as soon as I get up then."

"Good idee," nodded Mr. Creed as we all took our chairs.

Once again, it was like as if somebody else was there a-spying on us, maybe from just at the open door. I turned, but I saw nothing. Then I ate, and enjoyed it, the way I mostly enjoy to eat.

The talk went on while we ate. Mr. Creed told me things about the Voths; how they were standoffish, no ways neighborly; how they kept up their old, old house well, but never farmed, never even gardened. They seemed to have money enough to live without working. Which made it all the more strange that they'd tried to fence off that little rocky tag of the Forshay land, had even started to bluff Mr. Creed out of it. Once or twice, folks had come close enough to their place to hear singing amongst the trees, songs in no language air fellow in the Wolter Mountain country knew of. And the two chimneys at the two ends of their stone house now and then gave off odd-looking smoke, with green and pink and yellow sparks in it.

"They've lived round here just long enough for folks to tell one another that nobody knows what they're up to, or why they're up to it," Mr. Creed wound up talking as he wound up eating. "Just now, I reckon that whatever it is, it ain't nothing good for the right kind of folks hereabouts. John, I hope you can help us decide about that. In your life, you've come against a right much of things that might could help."

"I'll be right glad to do what I can," I said, laying down my fork. "Just now," and I got up, "I think I'll go up that trail and maybe learn something in a nice way."

"Think you should?" growled Mr. Creed.

"Seems to me the best thing to do."

"I'll go along, John," offered Luke.

"No, just me," I said. "So far, probably they don't figure me as on your side." I took my guitar under my arm. "This will make me look peaceable. Maybe they'll talk for me to listen."

A-going out, again I had that being-looked-at feeling near at hand, but didn't see a thing. It was like that all across the hollow, dodging off when I looked round. But at the trail I felt nothing like that. I had a sense of aloneness as I started the climb.

Being once up and down already, I didn't find the trip so nervish. I made good time up to the top. It seemed to me there were plainer monkey-faces here and there in Mr. Creed's rocks. Beyond was the slope with that big figure, and on the crest stood the Voth brothers.

I flung up a hand friendly-fashion, and started across the monkey-faced rocks and up the slope. They stood a-waiting. I took them to be men in their forties. From what Mr. Creed had described, I knew Brummitt Voth by his gaunted body and his fancy vest and hat, and Hooper Voth by his chunky build.

"Gentlemen," I hailed them, "I thought I'd come visit."

"Visit?" said Brummitt Voth after me. All four of their tin-colored eyes looked into me.

"My name's John," I made my introduction. "I was a-stopping by the Forshays, and I heard a couple of waif words about you all. Mr. Creed acted mad at first, now he thinks things can turn out all right with him and you. I thought I might could help, smoothing things betwixt neighbors."

"Are you a Forshay?" Brummitt Voth inquired.

"No, sir."

"Are you aught of kin?" asked Hooper Voth.

"None in this world," I said.

"Creed Forshay was a trifle emphatic about where we fenced our line," said Brummitt Voth. "We took out the fence. That should satisfy him." He fell silent a moment. "For now," he added on.

Hooper Voth eyed my guitar. "Are you a wandering bard?"

"I know Byard Ray the fiddler," I told him.

"No, I meant a bard—a minstrel. My brother and I love to hear old music, if it's old enough."

"I try to pick the oldest songs in the mountains." I

smiled my friendliest. "A-going here and there in these mountains, a-carrying my guitar with the silver strings."

"Silver," Hooper Voth said. "Don't you carry more than that?"

"Sometimes a spare shirt and socks," I told him. "Mostly, just the guitar, and trust to God for what I need else."

"Trust to God," said Brummitt Voth after me. "Is he in these mountains?"

"I hear tell he's everywhere, and these mountains are full of wonder. I recollect names like Ugly Bird and One Other, and the Gardinel and the Behinder."

"That's impressive," said Brummitt Voth, like as if he knew of those names. "Now, Mr.—"

"I just go by John," I said. "All I hope is, I've got some of the goodness of others who've had the name."

"I like the way he talks, Brummitt," said Hooper Voth, like as if I wasn't there to be reckoned on. "He might turn out a friend."

"I'm glad you think so," I spoke up, and didn't add that this sounded different from those who called the Voths standoffish.

They queried me things, standing there. I told some of what I'd seen and done in the mountains. If they didn't believe, they showed no disbelief. Brummitt Voth acted double interested when I told of seeing Devil Anse Hatfield risen from his grave by a spell sent across time.

"John might be a stimulus to some of our efforts, Hooper," said Brummitt Voth in his clipped way.

"I think the same, brother Brummitt," said Hooper Voth. "A practical help. If he's a peacemaker for Creed Forshay, he can take back a message that we accept the judgment on that small tract." He snickered, though I didn't see the joke. "For the time being."

"You all pointed out to him, not much of a pay crop could grow there," I said. "So you all shouldn't much value it your own selves."

They'd turned to go the other side of the ridge, betwixt dark pine and oak and hickory in bunchy thickets, with vines grown among them. I went along. It wasn't far on a mossy little trail to their place, the old house the Gibb family had lived in so long.

That house was solid-made, of such rocks as come off a hillside, fitted by a master fitter. You could hardly make out the plaster that held them. Without my poking close, I judged that plaster had been mixed long ago, worked together of clay and water and lime, such lime as is burned out of limestone. The stuff would have come to be as hard as the rocks it bound.

The windows were of smaller stones. Their glass was in iron frames on hinges bolted in. Behind the panes hung brown linen curtains. One curtain looked to have something inside, a shadow on it, with a bunchy head set low and forward on not much of a neck. The roof, as Mr. Creed had told it to me, was of flat pieces of shale, laid like slates. At each end rose up a chimney.

And in front grew a big old oak, old maybe as the house, with its broad branches shading the roof.

"Whoever ran up that house knew what he was doing," I said.

"Old ways can be the best ways," said Brummitt Voth, taking off his hat. The fair hair had died away in the front, so that he looked to have a fine, wide, thinking brow.

"It's stone-floored and stone-walled inside," he said. "The only wood is in the roof beams—seasoned so hard these two centuries, you couldn't drive a nail into it."

I looked at something else. Against one end chimney leaned a big woven figure. It was twined out of long shoots and dried-up vines, like basketwork, and it stood maybe twelve feet tall and more than half that much wide and deep. Its shape was rough human, with long, long arms that put me in mind of the stone figure on the slope back yonder.

"You survey that image rather fixedly, John," said Hooper Voth.

"I'm admiring it," I said. "Who made it?"

"We did," he said.

"You gentlemen are clever with your hands," I praised them.

"Come into our house, John," said Brummitt Voth, grinning his fine, white teeth. "We'll make you a cup of tea, though Americans don't generally relish tea."

"No," I agreed him. "We thought so little of it one time, we flung a whole shipload of it into Boston Harbor up north."

Gentlemen, you should ought to have heard them laugh.

"John's an original wit," said Hooper Voth at last. "Come in and sit down, John."

"Thank you kindly, but I'll go back down and tell the Forshays things are settled betwixt them and you all," I said.

"Or on the way to a decisive settlement," Brummitt Voth said, almost like as if he was putting me straight.

Like a shot, I made up my mind to something. "I'll come back if you don't mind," I said, "and maybe fetch a friend who can appreciate all this."

"Bring him, if he's as agreeable as you," Brummitt Voth granted me.

"It's a lady, and she has more education than I have. She's interested in old, old things, she can talk to you about them."

"All right," said Hooper Voth. "Bring her."

Going, I felt them watch me. I walked among their dark, viney trees and down their slope and took the trail below. When I got to the low ground of the Forshay property, I felt something that hadn't been up on the mountain, that I'd half forgotten about.

I mean the sense of being watched by something that wouldn't let me see it. I took the feeling all the way to the cabin. Mr. Creed and Luke were interested to hear all I brought to tell.

"Now, sir," I said to Mr. Creed, "you've made me welcome here, and I hope you'll let me ask somebody else to come."

"Air friend of yours can stay with us, John," he said right off.

"Her name's Holly Christopher," I told him. "She's been educated in special things at the University, she's known through the land for her study of folklore. I've cut her trail now and then, and sometimes we've given each other knowledge."

"Will she be all right here?" asked Luke. "We live in simple ways, and perhaps some choosy old lady—"

"I don't reckon she's older than you, Luke," I said. "A-studying what she does, she's not persnickety about where she stays. And by the way, she's a right pretty woman."

"Does she know she's pretty?" inquired Mr. Creed.

"She'd be a fool not to know, and she's no fool. But she also knows that being pretty isn't enough to run air show on earth by itself. I like her, and so will you if you let her come."

Mr. Creed said, "Go ahead," and I got on their country telephone and put through a call to a Chapel Hill number. After while, "Hello," came Holly's voice, a low voice with music to it.

"This is John, Holly. Up in the Wolter Mountain country."

"John, how good to hear you. What are you doing up there? Something to interest me?"

"Maybe," I replied her, and went on to say some things about the Forshays and the Voths, and the place on the mountain that had belonged to the family of Jonathan Gibb.

"Gibb?" she said the name after me. "Gibb, did you say? Oh, that's marvelous, John. Listen, today I just finished with a seminar here at the University. I'll be in my car at sunrise tomorrow morning. How long is it up there?"

"No more than six hours, driving carefully. I'd say, come to Sky Notch and you'll be met. There's a filling station at Sky Notch—Duffy Parr runs it. I'll look for you there round about noon."

She vowed she'd come, and we hung up.

After supper, Mr. Creed called again for music. I picked and sang a couple he could recollect way back to when he was little, "Mathy Groves" and "The Death of Queen Jane." Luke tuned his banjo and we played some things together. That pleased Mr. Creed in special.

"I'm glad for my boy to relish good old things," he said. "I figure he's the smartest Forshay by the name, and I've always wanted the best for him. I got him a good college education—no, devil be damned, I nair got it for him. He worked his own way through Shenstone College, but I stood back of him in that. Now he's got learning, and he's got love of this land, and I'm proud for him."

Luke's handsome face grinned. He'd rather have his daddy speak well of him than air other man on earth.

Finally we were ready to sleep. I had the loft room, going up there by a ladder, and a candle because there was no electricity. Luke made me up some blankets on an old army cot in the loft and said good night. I took off my clothes and blew out the candle and stretched myself down to close my eyes.

But I wished I didn't keep a-feeling that something was there in the loft with me, maybe humped over at the foot of the cot or a-hanging to the rafters like a big bat. I told myself that it was just only my fancy, but that made it worse. No luck, gentlemen, being bothered with what's not there—better maybe for it to be there so you can do something about it. I hated that kind of sneaky company in the dark. All the things Mr. Creed had said about the Voths and the Gibbs before them, and some of the things the Voths had said their own selves, made them sound like folks with the very sort of power I'd hated and fought against for all my years. Now and then, I'd been able to see such people with such powers fall and be brought down to nothing, and their place knew them no more. But also I knew right well that there was still another sight of evil, strong and mighty, to face in this world.

A-thinking I'd do well to stay awake, I dropped off to sleep and didn't stir hand or foot till I heard Luke and Mr. Creed a-clattering round below me to make coffee and fry eggs for breakfast.

III

Just before noon, I got into the Forshay pickup truck with Luke and we took off for Sky Notch, round about ten miles away, next to Dogged Mountain. We got there to find Holly Christopher in her little red car, a-waiting for us at the filling station. She jumped out and grabbed me by both my hands.

"John, John," she cried out at me, and gave me a kiss. "It's good to see you, it's always good to see you."

"Holly Christopher," I said, "let me make Luke Forshay known to you."

Luke's blue eyes bugged out to stare at her, and air man worth the name might could be forgiven for staring. Holly was a pure down fine-looking young woman, a little taller than the common height, and slim and sweet in her figure in brown slacks and brown jersey top. Round her neck hung a little sort of blue thing on a thin leather cord. Her face was as fine-cut as if some master jeweler had done it on one of those stones they call cameos. Her eyes were as dark as two pools deep in the shade of the forest. And she had soft-tanned cheeks and a mouth red and ripe. Her hair showed the Indian blood she could claim. It was shiny black and straight, cut short and sort of chubby to her head, with square bangs in front. The hand she gave Luke was long and slim, with a ruby ring on it.

"I'm glad to know a friend of John's," she smiled.

"And I'm right glad to know you, Miss Christopher," said Luke, meaning it all the way down to where he lived.

"If we're to be friends, you call me Holly."

"Miss Holly," he said, his handsome face all pinked up.

"Holly," she told him again.

"Holly, then," he said after her, and let go her hand like as if he hated to. Then he turned to me, half-surprised to find out I was still there. "I'll drive back with her and show her how we get to our place," he said. "You can bring the pickup."

"I don't drive a car, Luke," I said, and he sort of squinched his face, the way they all do when I admit that. "You let me ride with Holly and come along with your own truck."

He nodded, though you could see he'd rather it was the other way round. I got in Holly's car with her and told her which way to get out on the country road to the Wolter Mountain neighborhood.

"And drive right carefully on these twisty turns," I gave her the advice.

"I will," she said. "Lots of people think they're expert speedsters the minute they get a little red car, but I'm not one of them. John, your friend Luke is a mighty fine-looking, mighty fine-mannered young man."

"The way I figure, he thinks as good as that about you," I said.

She asked me to build on what I'd said over the long-distance phone, and I told her again about meeting the Voths and how, after starting out to squabble with Mr. Creed Forshay, they'd pulled up the stakes for their fence and then acted friendly and clever with me. She harked at all I said, like as if it was a hundred dollars in her pocket to know about it.

"I'm so glad you asked for permission to bring me to meet them," she said. "But we'll talk more about my motives when I can explain it to our hosts, the Forshays. You haven't told me how you've been faring, and how things are with that lovely Evadare girl of yours."

"Evadare's a-stopping off with my friends, the Ramseys," I said. "I'm out a-picking up a little money owing me here and there, and we figure to get married before this month runs all the way out. I'd be at the Ramsey place to join her by now if all this Voth business hadn't boiled up."

We turned in on the Forshay driveway and swung round the edge of the fish pond toward the cabin and stopped by the stable.

"John," said Holly as she put on her brakes, "do you have a sort of sense that something is watching us?"

"I've had that sense yesterday, and today too," I said. "I thought I'd mentioned it to you."

Mr. Creed Forshay was by the door, a-smoking his corncob, and when I made the introductions he admired Holly with his wise eyes. "I'm beholden to John for a-fetching such a beauty-looking lady to my house," he said.

Luke came out of the truck and joined us. He and his daddy wondered Holly would she like some noon dinner, but she fetched from her car a hamper that had things she'd fixed before she left out of Chapel Hill. There were roast beef sandwiches and some cole slaw in a plastic container, and a bottle of red wine she called burgundy. It was a plenty for the whole four of us. We ate it together, out in the yard. Then Mr. Creed allowed he'd make his own room ready for Holly.

"There's a sort of sleeping place out over the stable shed, above the stall where once we used to keep a cow," he said. "I'll just spread my gear there."

"Not there, you won't," said Holly at once. "Call that place your guest house, and let me stay there. Luke can show it to me."

Luke was ready and more than ready to do that, or air thing she would bid him. He picked up her suitcase and tote bag and out they went. Mr. Creed watched them go.

"I've got it in mind that there walks a right fine-looking couple," he said to me.

"You and I won't quarrel about that," I said.

When the two of them got back to the house, they were chattering away like two old friends who'd gone to Sunday school together. "It's a fine room up there, fit for a royal princess," said Holly, radiant with her smile.

"Then possibly it's fit for you," said Mr. Creed. "Let's go in and sit down and talk about things."

"The first thing," Holly said as Luke held the door for her, "is that charm John says you brought down from your spring."

It was a-lying on the fireboard over the hearth, next to the clock. I gave it to Holly and she unwrapped my handkerchief, then dangled the thing from the chain and bent down to give it a study.

"My advice is to bury this object," she said. "Bury it deep, and let me pronounce some words over it."

"I've heard tell of such things," Mr. Creed began, "but—"

"Let Holly run this business just now," Luke broke in, one of the few times I ever heard him break in on a person a-talking.

"Yes, sir," I seconded him, for I recollected a-hearing tales of praying out a bad spell. "Where's the spade?"

Luke fetched it and we walked through the yard, Holly a-carrying the charm on its chain, just one finger hooked through. She led us to a cucumber tree and pointed down to its roots. Luke drove the spade in, drove it in again, until he'd gouged out a hole big enough to hold a bucket. She nodded without speaking and knelt down to put the thing inside on the bottom, with the chain fallen on top.

Then Luke filled the hole up again and stamped down the dirt with the heel of his boot. Mr. Creed fetched in a flat chunk of rock that put me in mind of the shales on the Voth house, and fitted this over. Holly bowed her head and whispered something like a prayer. When she looked up, her face had turned bright again.

"That feeling we've noticed here," she said. "As if we were being watched. It's gone now, isn't it?"

"I don't feel it no more," said Mr. Creed, and, "Nor I don't," said I.

We went back in the house and took chairs round the table.

"John knew enough to see that a cross on something like that wasn't a good symbol," said Holly. "Just as he told you, the cross set in the circle turns up in the magic of several ancient cultures. I judge that your spring wasn't poisoned, but that charm was planted beside it for you to find and bring home. With it here at your house, it became a focus for some way of keeping watch on you, spying on you."

"I'd thought the Voths had got done with a-spying or things like that against us," said Mr. Creed, frowning. "They done took up the fence they started, and sent word by John that all was good feeling betwixt them and us."

"No, sir, they didn't send word quite like that," I recollected. "They added on something about just for the time being."

"That's so," Luke offered his word. "My feeling is, we'd better not let down our guard for a moment."

"Luke has the right of that," said Holly, and he beamed over her words. "I seem to have come here for more than I bargained for."

"What might could you have been a-bargaining for, ma'am?" Mr. Creed wondered her.

"John mentioned a family named Gibb that's lived here

since Revolutionary times," she said, "and a family named Gibb has been one of my research projects since I read about it in my freshman year."

Mr. Creed told again the tale of the Gibb family on Wolter Mountain, down to Jonathan Gibb who'd lived in Mr. Creed's time, though he hadn't been much known to Mr. Creed or other neighbors. Holly jotted down some notes on a legal pad she'd brought.

"Nobody knows where them Gibbs come here from," Mr. Creed finished up.

"Just possibly I have a clue to that myself," said Holly. "It goes back to Scotland, in the time of William and Mary."

"The late eighteenth century," said Luke, and she cut her dark eyes at him and nodded.

"Certain matters were reported about a man named John Gibb, a shipmaster," she started out. "You can see his name in Patrick Walker's *Biographia Presbyteriana,* and in Walter Scott's book of *Witchcraft and Demonology.* If John Gibb was a shipmaster, he must have had some education and social standing, but his neighbors felt mistrust for him. He claimed to have certain special powers and he drew some people into a sort of cult. They brought out all their Bibles and burned them."

"No wonder his neighbors didn't like that," said Luke. "I've been told that most Scotsmen value their Bibles."

"His action was enough to get him thrown into jail," Holly went on, "and he had trouble with the prisoners there. They wanted to pray, but he howled like a wild animal until they had to hold him down and stuff a gag in his mouth. At last he was transported to the American colonies. I'm not quite sure where, but that often happened to convicts in those days."

"I've read about that, too," said Luke. "I reckon lots of us are descended from people like that."

"Important thing is, we're here now," allowed Mr. Creed. "The old folks would say, no point to worry about who was the father of such a son. Because mostly sons are better or either worse than their daddies."

"It strikes me that Gibb isn't too strange and scarce a name," I spoke up. "Though mostly it's spoken and written Gibbs."

"Old Jonathan Gibb and others of his blood got mad if they got called Gibbs," recollected Mr. Creed. "But what else about this other Gibb, John Gibb? You don't make him sound like the sort of John this John we got here is named for."

"John Gibb is said to have brought along whatever powers he had to the American colonies," said Holly. "Other settlers said he offered sacrifices to the devil, and the Indians were in awe of him. He died somewhere around 1720."

"And," said Luke, "you're of the opinion he left descent."

"According to some old letters I've seen, he did," nodded Holly. "Those descendants weren't any more popular with their neighbors than John Gibb before them. At last they moved out, and at just about the time of the Revolution they seem to have come here to this state—to these very mountains." She looked all round at us, those dark eyes snapping. "I would suggest that your Gibb people here were the great-great-grandchildren, in some degree, of John Gibb. I wish I could have met them."

"I'm sorry for your sake that old Jonathan Gibb is dead and gone, and a sure thing to wind up in hell," said Mr. Creed.

"I'm sorry, too. It might have been profitable to talk to him."

"He wouldn't have talked to you, ma'am," Mr. Creed said.

"I'll bet he would," Luke argued him. "I'd like to see the man, even an oddball like Jonathan Gibb, who wouldn't talk to Holly Christopher."

"Luke, you overwhelm me," she dimpled at him. It was the first time I'd noticed that Holly Christopher had dimples. "But," she said, "Jonathan Gibb left behind him that house that John described to me. It sounds an unusual one."

"Ain't no other house like it hereabout," Mr. Creed told her.

"Tomorrow John will take me there to meet those new householders, the Voth brothers," said Holly. "But, gentlemen, this is all shoptalk on my part. I see John's guitar yonder, and isn't that a banjo in that case? My vote is for music."

"My vote's with yours," said Mr. Creed. "And I reckon I'll just pour us all a little thimbleful of how-come-ye-so."

He dug a fruit jar out from a cupboard and glasses. While Luke and I were a-tuning up, he poured out tots all round.

"Now, Holly Lady, that there blockade whiskey isn't like government run," he lectured at her. "I know the fellow who made it—him and me is cousins—and it's as clean as the cleanest. Nothing's touched it but the wood of the keg and the copper of the still and the glass of the jar. He keeps his equipment as clean as the galley of a flagship."

Luke and I picked up our drinks.

"I say a word of wisdom in time," warned Luke. "Just taste it, Holly, sip by sip. Don't put water in it, drink water for a chaser."

She tasted. "It's good," she said, and likely she meant it.

"Good?" Mr. Creed repeated her. "Why, you could bite this right off at the neck of the bottle."

We finished a-drinking one to another, and Holly asked me for one she'd heard me sing once, and joined in to help sing it:

> Poor Ellen Smith, as sweet as a dove,
> Where did she ramble, and who did she love . . .

When we'd done, Mr. Creed clapped us as loud as guns going off. "This here Holly girl sings like a bird in spring," he cried out. "I've been a-wanting to ask, what's that you wear round your neck?"

She held it out on its leather string. We saw it plain now. It was of blue stone, turquoise as I guessed, and it had been carved and polished into the shape of an elephant as big as your thumb—trunk, ears, all about it.

"It's Indian," she said. "My grandmother was a Cheyenne. She got that from a medicine man of some Arizona tribe, and she gave it to me."

"Looks oldish," said Mr. Creed, admiring it.

"Thousands of years old," Holly told him.

He cocked up his eyebrows. "How come the Indians to know about elephants thousands of years ago?"

"They had them here, Papa," said Luke. "Only they were really mammoths and mastodons. Their bones have been found, dating back ten or fifteen thousand years, with the spear points of Folsom man among them."

"I ain't nair heard tell there was Indians that far back, neither," said Mr. Creed. "A preacher showed me a book one time that said they was the ten lost tribes of Israel or some such matter."

He looked at Holly, like as if she could explain, and she did her best.

"I don't believe it's ever been established how early man came to America," she said. "There was a study of tools found in California, and L. S. B. Leakey—he's one of the foremost authorities on prehistoric man—dated them at about seventy-five thousand years ago."

"I declare to never," said Mr. Creed, and Luke was a-taking it in too, and so was I.

"Some dare to go back to times before that," Holly said next. "A government geological survey team turned up other tools in Mexico, and said they might be two hundred fifty thousand years old—called it archaeologically unreasonable, but said it anyway."

"You make me think that America isn't such a new world, after all," I said.

"But two hundred and fifty thousand years, Holly," said Luke. "A quarter of a million years ago. That was before mankind."

"Well, before modern mankind, at least," Holly agreed him. "Before man as we know him today, as we are mankind today. More like the time of early Neanderthal man —the time, say, of whatever manlike giant left his jaw in that pit at Heidelberg."

I took all this in, only half understanding. Holly and Luke were the college folks there; what education I had was mostly on the spot here and there.

"It's wonderful talking over these things with you, Holly," said Luke, shaking his head. "A great privilege."

"But let's bring things to the present," said Holly, sort of a-making a sparkle at him. "And the future, too. John, you started to tell me about your Evadare girl."

I'm always glad to talk about Evadare. I said that the world lighted up when I saw her, and that we aimed to take some land near Haynie's Fork, where the neighbors already said they'd help us build. I'd farmed when I was a young chap, and I reckoned I could farm again. Evadare was the sweetest flower in all those mountains, I told them I thought. It was a plain fact that Luke enjoyed to hear me say such things, because once or twice he'd acted mournful about how Holly and I were such choice friends.

Time went on with the talk. We had us another sip or so of the good blockade. Finally Holly allowed that she'd cook us our supper.

"I'll vote my yes on that," said Mr. Creed. "Woman's cooking is better than by a man. I've already took a frying chicken out of the deep freeze."

Holly fixed herself a clean dish towel to be an apron, and she took a knife and jointed the chicken up. Then she put vegetable shortening and some country butter together in the skillet to melt. Meanwhile, Mr. Creed stirred up dough and cut it up for biscuits and set it in the oven. Luke opened a jar of home-canned kraut to heat, but he near about spilled it on his boot, a-looking at Holly where she fried that chicken the right brown. Luke had it bad, and no I reckon about it. What did old Shakespeare say one time? It's in a play I saw at Flournoy College. "'Whoever loved that loved not at first sight?'" And it seemed to me like as if Holly kept a-cutting her dark-shining eyes back at Luke.

It turned out to be an early supper, and a good one. We ate up air piece of the chicken, and the gravy went good on the biscuits. Holly said she should ought to have baked a pie or something, and Mr. Creed begged her not to kill us with too much kindness. We kept on with more talk about how long men had been in America, and how the old Indians had said the figure on the Gibb slope had been there before the first of their tribe had come.

"I keep on with thoughts about that figure, with its long arms and hunched shoulders," said Luke, buttering his last biscuit. "And to that I add what Holly said about traces of human, or almost human, people on this continent two hundred fifty thousand years ago. Neanderthal man was a stocky, stooped fellow who could play the star part in your bad dreams. Could he and his kin have come over from Asia, across that land bridge that used to be at the Bering Strait?"

Mr. Creed acted proud that his son could know enough to talk of such things. "There's them tales about the Bigfoot, up on the northwestern Canadian border," he said. "That big, hairy ape-thing they keep a-saying is in those woods. I've always figured it was about ninety per cent made up, but that leaves ten per cent that you can wonder if it's true."

Holly made a sort of shaky shrug with her shoulders. Luke, at least, thought she looked wonderful a-doing it.

"When I came here, I may have found even more than I bargained for," she said. "You could do a doctor's dissertation on these things, Luke. Have you thought of going into graduate work?"

He told her he'd thought mostly of football when he was at Shenstone, and gave her a play-by-play report on how he'd touchdowned one time as a tight end. She knew enough football to understand him and talk back at him. Mr. Creed took time to say something on one side to me.

"My boy Luke acts like as if he's got the squaw fever," he said so they couldn't hark at him. "This Holly girl seems all right, though."

"If I had a son Luke's age," I said, "I couldn't call for a better girl for him to have. If so be he could get her."

"There's always that," Mr. Creed said.

It had come on to dark, and all four of us did the dishes and stacked them on the shelves. I reckon we all had a reason for feeling good in special; I mean, no thought that we were being looked at, listened to, by something hidden out of sight. Luke and I got back to the guitar and banjo, and Holly sang a couple of songs with us. Her voice was sweeter than honey in the honeycomb. Finally, she said she'd relish some sleep. Luke got a lantern and saw her out to the stable, then came back.

"I swear, John," he said, "that's a right nice girl you fetched here to visit us. You know, when you mentioned her at first, I wondered if you had something a-going with her."

"Not Holly and me," I was glad for his sake to tell him. "You heard us a-talking about Evadare, and you know I'm a gone gump about her. Some later time, I want to fetch her for a visit here."

"You do that," Mr. Creed invited. "We'll make her welcome."

I climbed the ladder to the loft and put my candle on the old table. Sure enough, no black shadows bunched in corners, no wonder if something was there, a-holding its breath so you wouldn't know it was a-looking and a-harking at you. I told myself that when we buried the circle cross charm, we'd cut the line to that spy. And I wondered if the Voths knew what we'd done.

I slept, as sound as a black bear in the wintertime, and woke up at dawn to go out with Luke to the fish pond. We dropped lines and the trout in there swarmed and fought to get on our hooks. Back we fetched four big ones for breakfast, gutting and scaling them fast and rolling them in corn meal to fry. Holly was there to help. All four of us sat down to eat. Holly praised those fish like as if they were the best-tasting in the world, and for my part I figure they near about were.

Holly chased Luke and me out so that she could do the breakfast dishes. We walked to the cucumber tree where the charm had been buried. "Looky there," said Luke sharply, and he pointed.

Something had dug there in the night, maybe a-trying to gouge the thing out. We saw the rock had been shoved aside, and earth flung this way and that, but the hole wasn't opened all the way down. I knelt to take a close look.

"What sort of thing would dig here?" I asked.

Luke stooped beside me. "I see a print in the soft earth," he said. "It must have rested a paw there while it scooped with the other. Only—that's not the mark of a paw. It was made by a man's hand."

I studied it myself. A hand was what it was; I saw the thumb and the spread-out fingers. But, gentlemen, it was an almighty big hand, bigger than mine or Luke's. And it had another strange thing about it.

"You sharpen your eyes and you'll see it had claws," I said to Luke. "On the thumb and the fingers. Longer than air nail a man can have, and wider and stronger to dig in."

That was the fact, too. We went back to the house, where Holly and Mr. Creed were a-laughing over something while they stowed the dishes away. We brought them out and showed them what had gone on beside the cucumber tree while we slept.

"Why didn't it finish digging that thing up?" Mr. Creed wanted to know. "It must have got down almost to it."

"Perhaps the words I said were enough to prevent it," said Holly, in a voice that almost whispered.

Luke pointed out the claw marks on the finger marks. "Holly," he said, "that puts me in mind of what you told us last night, of how once there may have been things in America that weren't animals, but weren't men either, as yet."

Holly walked toward the house. I caught up with her.

"Now what?" I asked.

"Now we'd better go visit those brothers, the Voths," she replied me. "Go and see if I'm to be made as welcome as they told you I'd be."

IV

Mr. Creed looked like as if he was worried. "Youins dead sure you'll be all right up yonder?" he wondered us.

"Let's just hope so," I said. "Anyhow, those Voths sounded and acted polite when they bid me come back and fetch Holly along."

Luke frowned and hiked his big shoulders. "I wish I was coming along, but I can see why I mustn't," he grumbled. "Here, John, take this."

He held out a pistol, a thirty-eight S&W, but I shook my head.

"Don't reckon I will," I said, and took up my guitar. "This is better for the trip. It's more peaceful to look at."

"John," said Mr. Creed, "it takes half an hour or so to go up there, and another half hour to come back down. We'll say, another hour and a half for you to pay your visit to them Voths. Two and a half hours in all. If youins stay away much past that, I'll be on the phone to the sheriff to come help us look for you."

Luke nodded his head to that, but Holly shook hers. It stirred her black hair round her face.

"What sheriff would believe the things we're trying to find out here, Mr. Creed?" she asked, and smiled, though it didn't truly have the sound of a joke. "Come on, John."

They stood at the door and watched us head away.

Holly and I walked along the edge of the fish pond. There was a big fluttery bunch of fish to swim toward us, the way chickens come to a fence to be fed. I made out some bream, some bass, three or four fine trout.

"I wish we had some bread or something to throw to them," said Holly. "How friendly they are."

"If you drop a hook in, you'll get a bite right quick," I said. "Maybe not the biggest fish, but the best fighter. They'd fight one another to take the hook."

"There's some sort of parable to that thought," she said, not air way cheerfully. "How life gives you something you think is good and wholesome, and then uses it to yank you out of your world."

"Yes, ma'am," I agreed her.

Holly climbed the trail up the mountain right well. She hadn't done all her folklore studies in libraries and class-rooms. She admired the trees and flowers and toadstools, the way I'd done and still did. "At least I know what direction we're going," she said. "Look on that walnut trunk. Where the moss grows is the north side."

"Look all the way round and you'll see moss on all sides of it," I said. "There's no way to tell direction except by stars and by sun, and you've got to look at them different ways with the different seasons."

"However did you learn so much, John?"

"I learn things a little at a time," I replied her. "I'm still a-trying to learn, air minute. I look to learn something new today, and live to use it."

Both of us kept a-trying to feel if we were being watched, though we'd agreed not to talk too much about such things. The feeling wasn't there till we got to where that rocky patch was at the top.

"I see those ape faces on the stones," said Holly.

They were sure enough plain to see. Plainer than before. I recollected stuff I'd heard, things I'd read in books about what had gone on before history. How that monkeys hadn't been wild in this part of the earth, not air that science knew of. No Indian air saw a monkey till white men fetched them from the old country for shows. And the rocks we stood over looked to have had that monkey face since the first days of this world.

Holly gazed up past the monkey faces to the slope. That big thing of rocks up there looked to be halfway bucking the knees of its short legs, halfway lifting its long, long arms at us.

"John," she said, "you could go all through America and not see anything like that. I've never exactly seen the like, even abroad; but it reminds me of certain things in England."

"What certain things you mean, Holly?" I inquired her.

"Figures on hills, cut into the turf down to where the chalk shows through in white lines," she said. "Such as the Long Man on Windover Hill in Sussex. And one like it, at Cerne Abbas in Dorset. And what they call Gogmagog, near Cambridge."

"Gogmagog," I repeated her. "There's something about Gog and Magog in the Book of Revelation."

"Gog and Magog became one name," she said. "It was in England before ever the Book of Revelation was written."

"Come on," I said. "We go up this-a-way to get to where the Voths live."

They weren't a-waiting for us, or if they were we didn't see them. But I recollected the way and found it, though it wasn't just exactly what I'd followed before.

The trees crowding from both sides somehow didn't look like the same trees. Those trees watched us, whether the Voths watched us or not. I recollect one that flung out its branches like the arms on something deep down under sea, waiting to grab and eat up something else. Another had vines all over it, drawn close like the wings of a roosting buzzard. And once, in the bark of a big, big pine, I made out what looked like a door put in there. I wasn't a-going to mention that to Holly, but that same second she saw it too. "A door there," she said, close to my ear. "But no catch. No knob. No latchstring out, to mean welcome. Nobody can get in, but what's inside can come out."

"If it comes out, maybe it leaves the door open to get back in," I said. "The open door policy, you might could say."

"Let's go ahead," she said, and she went ahead, faster than she'd been a-going so far.

We got to where we made out the house where the Voths lived, in amongst the trees, not so much hidden amongst them as hiding there.

"Here we are," I said, and lifted up my voice. "Hello! Hello, the house!"

"Hello yourself," came a voice back. From around one of the dark-stony corners walked Brummitt Voth.

He had off his hat, to show how his head was balded in front. "Welcome, John," he said. "I take it that this is the lady you said you'd bring to call on us."

His brother Hooper showed at the front door, under the wide, dark branches of the oak. I spared a look for the drawn curtain in the window beside the door. That shadow was in the curtain, where it had been before.

"Miss Holly Christopher," I said, "let me make you acquainted with Mr. Brummitt Voth and Mr. Hooper Voth. They allowed they'd be glad for you to visit them, talk to them, hark at things they know."

Their pale eyes were a-looking at Holly, half ready to eat her up. However different from folks the Voths were, they were like all men when they looked at Holly.

"We are honored Miss Christopher," said Brummitt Voth, a-putting up a hand to his brow like as if to take off the hat that wasn't there. And he said something past his shoulder to his brother, in a language I'd nair heard before.

I maybe frowned, because that's not what a man might call good manners. Brummitt Voth saw, and made a smile at me.

"Hooper and I sometimes talk in that jargon, John," he said. "I remarked that I was glad that Miss Christopher had found her way here."

"*Misle gran ches tarer,*" Holly came out with the same talk. "A traveler knows the way, gentlemen."

Their mouths dropped open about a foot with surprise, and Brummitt Voth hit his both hands together. "You speak the *Shelta Thari!*" he cried. "This is wonderful past counting, Miss Christopher."

"*Shelta Thari,* the tinker's language," she said. "I've read Ignatius Donnelly's book, and I've spoken with tinkers in England. I wonder if John Bunyan didn't know *Shelta Thari.*"

"Maybe he knew it, and then forgot it," said Hooper Voth, and tried another string of the strange words at her.

"You're a-leaving me out in the cold, folks," I said. "I don't talk air language but just a little countrified English."

"On our brief acquaintance, I've heard you speak very much to the point, John," said Brummitt Voth, a-smirking. "But let's stick to a tongue we all can understand. We're glad you came, and we wonder what profit we can give you."

"Just conversation, Mr. Voth," said Holly. "This house of yours," and she gave it her look, "it's so wonderfully built. I'm sure you feel happy in it."

I looked, too. I had a sense that something moved up in those oak tree branches, amongst their darkest shadow. I couldn't see it, but I had a notion it was about a man's size and not quite a man's shape. I couldn't make it out the way I might have if it would move into the light.

The Voth brothers were glad about Holly a-being there, and no I-reckon about it. They smiled at her, moved close to her; if they'd had a little bitty bit more nerve they'd have put hands on her. I was double glad that Luke Forshay wasn't with us, because likely he'd have hit one of those brothers, or even both, and then what? But I wasn't on top of Wolter Mountain to wonder such things. Not right then and there.

There at the end of the house, they helped Holly look over that big shape wickerworked out of branches and vines.

"That's artistically done," she praised it. "It reminds me of woven figures I've seen in England."

"England?" they both repeated her. "Oh, yes, you've been to England."

"Twice. In a hall there they had those big, baskety old giants on display. One of them was Corineus, the chief of the British giants that Brutus fought and overcame."

"Corineus was on Brutus's side," said Brummitt Voth. "Not on the side of Albion."

"Excuse me, I was mistaken there. The other giant in that hall was Gogmagog, the British giant. He had a staff with a globe full of spikes, fastened to it with a chain. The deadliest flail I ever saw."

I had walked past them toward the rear of the house. For the first time I saw a stone shed back there, all open on the side toward me. A forge was there, anvil and hearth and bellows. On the anvil lay something that shone pale. Out in front was an old, old plow, turned upside down. Its share was rusty and its handles worn with use in the field.

Holly came to look, too. "And you do metalwork as well as basketwork," she said. "You gentlemen are so gifted, so informed."

"It's a blessing to work with the hands," said Brummitt Voth, like somebody a-saying a text in church. "We're trying to make a new share for that plow we bought second-hand in Sky Notch."

Holly went into the shed. They went with her. I stood outside to watch.

"But this is silver work," she said.

"Exactly," said Brummitt Voth, rubbing the share with his hand. "We want to use silver, not iron, if we plow ourselves a little plot to grow vegetables."

"Why not use the iron plow?" she asked, sweetly as a song.

The brothers were both quiet a moment. Then Brummitt Voth nodded at Hooper Voth, like as if to tell him to do the talking.

"This may sound strange to you, Miss Christopher," said Hooper Voth, cracking a silly-looking grin. "It may sound even superstitious, fatuous. But when we took this land, the family that had owned it made certain stipulations. One of these was, the earth here is not to be dug or stirred with any iron tool."

"How interesting," said Holly, and her dark eyes shone. "Did they say why not?"

"It seems to be an old, old belief in this part of the country," he said to her. "If you use iron in this earth, it will bring a storm of rain and thunder and lightning. Wash you away."

"Again this reminds me of old England," she said. "It's like a belief there used to be, is still mentioned in Scotland and Wales. I mean the *Sith Bhruaith.*"

Both of those brothers hiked up their ears when she spoke that name, the way they'd done when she talked the talk they called *Shelta Thari.*

"*Sith Bhruaith,*" Brummitt Voth said after her. "You know about that. So do we."

"Oh, in English, the Goodman's Croft," said Holly.

"I've heard tell about places called that in these mountains," I felt like putting in. "A piece of land let go to trees and brush and so on, for the spirits. They say you call Satan the Goodman, so as not to rile him. But I've had it in mind that maybe old, old gods were thought to be good in their day."

"What philosophical acumen, John," said Hooper Voth, a-giving me a grin. "You have a good sense of things, I daresay. But, since both of you are so flatteringly interested, let me go on to explain. Before the first white settler came here to build this solid old stone house, this tract was sacred to the gods of the Indians. They, too, never farmed it—and I've heard that the old Indians were good farmers. Their wishes seem to have been courteously respected by the family that settled here."

"What family was that?" Holly inquired him, like as if she didn't know already.

"Gibb was the name," said Brummitt Voth. "We never really knew them and, as I believe, the last Gibb has died. But we accepted their stipulation about the land. We try to be honest men."

The three walked out of the blacksmith shed together.

"Come into our house," Brummitt Voth invited us. "We consider the pair of you welcome here, the more so because you're helping to compose things with our neighbors, the Forshays. We have some things that may prove interesting."

I was interested to go inside, anyway. We went into a big room, all the way from front to back of the house. Overhead showed those wooden rafter beams, black as iron with the age on them. The floor was laid of flat stones, like a pavement, and on it stretched out a couple of bearskin rugs, maybe left there by Jonathan Gibb. The furniture was heavy-made of oak, the chairs had leather cushions. I judged they'd come from far away and likely had cost something once. There were shelves against the walls, also made of flat stones. I saw books on them, dark books with a sneaky look to them somehow. Midway of the room was a fireplace, but no fire in it, nor yet a look of a fire there any time lately. I felt a sort of creep inside me, but Holly smiled her pretty smile. She walked to the hearth and studied something on the fireboard. It was a curve of bright blade that shone yellow in the light from that window where the shadow showed on the curtain, but looking from inside like as if the shadow was cast from outdoors.

"A golden sickle," she said.

"Not exactly golden, Miss Christopher," said Brummitt Voth, a-standing just about as near to her as he dared. "Gold plate over bronze. It's an antique, maybe two thousand years old."

She half put out her hand to it, but drew it back. "Interesting," she said. "Evocative."

"Evocative of what?" Hooper Voth asked.

"More than anything, of an opera with that sort of sickle in it," Holly said. "*Norma*, by Bellini. They presented it last winter in New Orleans. Do you gentlemen know *Norma?*"

"We've heard *Norma*, yes," said Hooper Voth. "What

does *Norma* mean to you, Miss Christopher, I mean in particular?"

"The music, the beautiful music," she said at once. "That duet with Norma and Adalgisa, 'Mira Norma.'" Her tuneful voice sang a few lines in Italian. I touched my guitar's silver strings to pick up the melody. She sang it over, in English this time:

Hear me, Norma, before thee kneeling—

Then she broke off. "I don't have the voice for it," she said.

"You've a voice to sing with the gods of music," vowed Brummitt Voth. "I agree with you, it's a splendid opera, though perhaps not exactly true to historical fact."

"It has a happy ending, more or less," put in his brother, and that sounded strange to me, for I'd heard tell a grand opera isn't grand unless it's unhappy at the finish.

"Will you and John stay for luncheon?" asked Brummitt Voth.

"I'd love to, but I don't eat at noon," said Holly. "I have to watch my figure, you know."

The both of them were a-watching her figure, and I didn't reckon either one of them saw aught wrong with it. Brummitt Voth took a step nearer. He had a hand up, like as if to take hold of her. But then he backed that step's length away again.

"What are you wearing around your neck?" he croaked.

"This?" She took it in her fingers and held it out. "Just a curious old Indian pendant."

"An elephant," said Hooper Voth, not happy about it. "A strange thing for Indians to make. Elephants and Indians hardly go together, do they?"

"I never thought of that," Holly said, though of course I knew different. "But whatever it is, it's nothing wonderful

46

compared to this fine old house of solid stone, and all the things you're doing. Your own work, I should guess, is a great reward to you."

"We're happy with what we find to do," said Hooper Voth. "Our work and our studies—they're rewarding, as you say. Twenty times beyond our hopes."

Brummitt Voth shot him a look, like as if there was something wrong about saying that. We all went out again.

They made their good-byes to Holly, while I stood under the branches of the oak tree and tried not to look up into them at what moved itself round in them. I dared only one quick peek. I had a sense of something my size or thereabout, dark-colored; but whether it had fur like an animal or scales like a snake, I didn't make out. I did think it could take grip with its feet as well as its hands. I wished it didn't hang right over me.

"Please come again," Brummitt Voth was a-telling Holly. "It's a great pleasure to talk with someone so well informed."

"We'll see to your coming again," Hooper Voth gave his second to that. "We won't take no for an answer."

"Good-bye, gentlemen," I said, stirring some bit of music out of my guitar. "You all come see us."

"Just possibly we shall," said one or other of them.

We walked off on the woodsy path. It was like a-being somewhere amongst folks that strained their ears to hear what you might say.

"John," said Holly, "you said you'd join Evadare after this visit to the Forshays."

I knew what she meant; no talk of what we'd been into, not with air bush and air rock more or less crowded close, with whatever passed with them for ears all cocked up to hear us.

I talked some about our wedding plans and the house we'd build at Haynie's Fork. Holly mentioned how she'd seen some pretty cloth Evadare had woven on her loom, and would Evadare do some like that and maybe sell to people? I said, no doubt she would. Then I tried to banter her a trifle about how Luke Forshay liked to be round with her, but she turned the subject to something else.

We came to the slope with the figure on it, and went down across the rocky patch. The ape-faces showed plainer still than they'd been, so plain I took care not to set my foot on any. Beyond that, we started down the steep trail. Even there, it was a feel of watchers and listeners.

"Name the flowers we see growing here, John," said Holly, to make sure we didn't talk of what we hadn't better talk of, not there and then.

That was right smart of her, I knew. So, step by step down along that narrow, snaking way, I showed her the flowers, and she carried on about how pretty they were. You'd have reckoned that's what we'd come out to see, the flowers.

A tawny tuft of cotton grass where sun struck down; spiderwort; wake-robin; a late, pale Indian cucumber blossom; and some turkey beard round a pine, part of it chewed off by a deer or something.

There was a rattle and scuttle amongst some weeds right where we stopped to look at the turkey beard. "Is that a squirrel?" Holly inquired me, and I said, "I reckon," though it was too big a noise for a squirrel—too big for either a groundhog, when it came to that. I wondered if I wished to know just exactly what it was.

Toward the bottom of the trail down, colic root and bunchflowers, and Holly allowed they were right pretty, too.

Neither one of us mentioned one time even, the sense of something a-going along with us, close to us, its weight on us, the way the air weighs just before one pure hell of a blow of wind and rain.

This time the sense stayed with us when we got to the Forshay place, along past the fish pond where now the fish hung at the bottom of the water. And all the way to the cabin, with Mr. Creed and Luke a-coming out of the door, glad to see us back.

V

"Thank the good Lord youins both got back safe," Mr. Creed hollered us, his face all shiny with a big smile. "We been a-holding our breath for you."

Luke was just before a word of his own, but Holly put her gold-tanned forefinger to her mouth; and that mouth was a lighter red than usual, I saw. She wanted silence all round. Straight to her car she went and opened the door and then the glove compartment, and took out a folded paper. Then she fairly ran to the house and inside. She spread the paper out on the table. It was written in words of black ink. She beckoned for us all to come ring round with her. We did so, not speaking a word.

"Say your Christian name," she said, pointing at Mr. Creed.

He blinked, but, "Creed," he said.

She pointed again. "Luke," said Luke, and her finger came round to me.

"John."

"Holly," she spoke her own name. "Now, listen as I read."

Standing at her shoulder, I looked at the paper while she said the words of it, solemn as a prayer:

"All ye things and spirits of evil, I forbid you this house and home; I forbid you, in the three holy names, our blood and flesh, our bodies and souls; I forbid you all the nail holes in this house and home, until you have traveled over every hillock, waded through every water, till you have counted all the leaflets of the trees and counted all the starlets in the sky, until that beloved day arrives when heaven comes upon this earth."

At the bottom of the writing I saw three crosses in a row:

† † †

Still holding up her hand for quiet, Holly read it through again, and one time more, making three. At last she smiled at us all, one after another.

And that heavy sense was gone from out the air on all sides of us.

"I think that's going to work," she said, with the smile. "Now, in this house, we can't be overheard or attacked. We can talk about what's been done, and what perhaps we can do ourselves."

We all sat down. I, anyway, felt tired, but a trifle easier.

"What's that there thing you read out?" Mr. Creed inquired her.

"It's a form of spell credited to Albertus Magnus," Holly told him. "I was present once in a home in the Pennsylvania Dutch country, where it was read the way I just read it, to drive out some witchcraft. I asked for a copy and they wrote it out for me and told me to keep it with me all the time. And I've kept it."

"Albertus Magnus," said Mr. Creed. "I've got it in mind, he wrote a bad book of magic one time, didn't he?"

"What they call the *Grand Albert*," I said. "I've been up against that in my time."

"It's hard to decide on all the legends about Albertus Magnus," said Holly. "I've had a try at coming to what facts are known. He was born in a town on the Danube in

1205, and he was considered one of the foremost scientific philosophers of his day."

"He must have been a great one to be called Albertus Magnus," Luke said.

"Oh," she said, smiling, "that's just the Latin form of his Germanic name, Albrecht de Groot. But he was a priest, he was a bishop of the Church, and Saint Thomas Aquinas was his pupil. And what he left behind as a formula of exorcism seems to have cleared the air in this house, wouldn't you say?"

"I feel better," I said for myself. "I even feel a little small bit hungry."

"Hungry," Mr. Creed repeated me. "Let's eat up a little something or other."

It wasn't any great shakes, I suppose. We made sandwiches of peanut butter, and Holly asked that we have some blockade whiskey. It was plain that she felt the need of something to hike her up.

While we ate, she talked, and made me talk. I told in particular about that glimpsing of some sort of thing a-moving in the shadows of the oak branches in front of the Voth house.

"That's what I felt, or maybe saw, and if John saw it too, it was there," said Holly. "This isn't an unusual story, gentlemen. There are tree spirits, bush spirits, in the legends of all sorts of peoples in every part of the world."

"But what about the one the Voths have in their oak tree?" Mr. Creed wondered us. "That there's more or less a new thing."

"Or an old thing," said Holly. "I was thinking again of Reginald Scot's book, and the list he made of frightening spirits—Kit-with-the-candlestick and the spoorn and so on, and the Man in the Oak." She looked round at us, serious as at a funeral. "There's been the Man in the Oak in all sorts of places. And that's not all we have to worry us, up there on Wolter Mountain."

"What's the main real trouble?" Luke asked her.

"I talked with them, and I think I know the answer to that." She weighed air word as she spoke. "We're up against Druids and Druidism."

"Druidism," I said after her. "How bad is that?"

"I've heard tell, off and on, about Druids," said Mr. Creed. "It was in the county seat paper, Halloween time one year. They was supposed to be some kind of beardy old-time priests, ain't that a fact?"

"Only part of the fact," replied Holly. "There was more to a Druid than a sort of Santa Claus in a long robe with a bunch of mistletoe in his hand."

"They worshiped nature," spoke up Luke.

"Yes," said Holly, "but the old magazine advertisement spoke the truth about nature in the raw being seldom mild. A lot of half-romantic foolishness has been said and written about Druids. They've been described as noble savages. But they weren't savages—not when they had metalwork and grew crops and built stone temples. And they weren't particularly noble either, not with bloody human sacrifices to their gods of nature."

"No," Luke agreed her.

"Part of the noble-savage attitude comes from the fact that the Druids left no writings we know of. The Celts in Gaul and Britain understood writing—we have inscriptions on stone, in Greek or Roman letters, before Caesar's conquests. But the Druids don't seem to have committed rituals or records to writing. They always passed these on orally, from old priests to young ones."

"That esoteric?" said Luke.

"Or that secretive," she said. "It was usually a Roman commentator who wrote anything down. We're in obscurity about the real names of their gods. They had a god named Los, and a goddess Vala, we think. And of course, their real chief deity was Baal."

"Baal," echoed Mr. Creed. "That's in the Bible. The Philistines had Baal."

"And the Carthaginians and the Gauls," went on Holly. "The worship of Baal reached all over the world from Persia to Ireland. It's still heard in place names— Balquhidder in Scotland, or Byron's haunted Bridge of Balgownie. And Baltimore."

"Baltimore?" said Mr. Creed. "Over here?"

"Baltimore in Maryland is named for the town in Ireland. I've heard that the name comes from *Bal-tigh-more*, the grove of the great god Baal."

She stopped to let us drink in that much. Then she went on ahead.

"That Man in the Oak, in front of that strange stone house," she whispered. "How good a look did you get at it, John?"

"About enough to wonder myself about it," I had to confess. "It looked as big as a man or a bear; and its shape might could have been something like man-shape. I can't rightly say if it had fur or feathers or scales, but it was one of the three. And it must have had what you might call fingers on its toes, it could take a grip with its feet."

"Like what the Ashantis in Africa call Sasabonsam," said Holly. "He lives in a silk cotton tree there, and catches unwary men with his feet as they pass below."

"Might that be suggested by great apes?" asked Luke. "Gorillas?"

"Who knows?" said Holly. "The thing in that oak was no gorilla, it was something worse. Gentlemen, the oak was the Druid's sacred tree, for good and evil. They said it beckoned the lightning and thunder. It has age and size and strength beyond other trees. And they made bloody sacrifices to their oak-spirit." She trembled in her throat. "I'll come to those sacrifices in a minute. It's horrible to think about what reminded me of them."

She got out paper and spread it on the table and took a pen.

"We'd better put down notes about this," she said. "See what we have to face."

She dashed off several lines about what we'd said so far.

"Didn't the Druids build Stonehenge in England?" Luke asked her.

"No, that was about four thousand years ago," she told him. "There weren't even Celts in England then, much less Druids. Though there's a lot of do-it-yourself legendry about how old the Druids are. Henry Rowlands wrote his *Mona Antiqua Restaurata* in 1723 or thereabouts—I sound like someone taking doctor's orals—and he says that Noah's sons were Druids and began a religion that Rowlands called 'pure and untainted.' Somebody else claims Gomer, the son of Japheth, as the founder of Druidism."

"If it's the oak-tree religion, that's all through the world. The Indians had it, and I recollect hearing the Romans did."

"The Romans hated the Druids for their human sacrifices," said Holly. "Julius Caesar felt that was horrible, though his own Roman people hadn't given up human sacrifice until about a century before. And Pliny scolds the Druids. The Romans wiped them out in old Britain, because they felt it must be done."

"Suetonius Paulinus massacred them on Mona—the Isle of Man," said Luke. "They were there with priestesses in black robes, waving torches and howling curses, when the Romans came across to fight them."

Holly blinked at him. Her smile came back to admire him. "How did you know about that, Luke?"

"Why," he said, a-smiling back, "it's in Tacitus. We studied Tacitus in our ancient history classes at college."

For a moment there was that bright feeling betwixt him and Holly. It almost drove out the trouble-haunting in the room. But the moment went away, and she turned back to what we had to figure out there.

"I knew the Voth brothers were into Druidism, almost at once," she said. "They talked to each other in the *Shelta Thari*, and when I spoke it too they seemed to be delighted. That's a language spoken sometimes amongst wandering tinkers, but it's been traced to the priestly caste of the Druids among the ancient Celts. It was part of Druid secrecy, to make their religion powerful, to rule over even the chiefs and kings of Gaul and Britain. And there at their house was direct evidence, to confirm the spoken evidence."

"What evidence, child?" asked Mr. Creed.

"They had a giant figure of wickerwork," she said. "Many times the size of a human being. That's one of the most important and the most ghastly items in the Druidic rites. Such a wickerwork figure was used as a cage. They'd put their victims into it and burn them alive for a sacrifice to their tree gods and nature gods. No wonder even those tough Roman legionaries turned sick."

"Turned sick," said Luke after her, "and afraid. They were afraid of the magic on that British isle. Remember the story of the Argonauts. They sailed their *Argo* ship through inland seas—the Black and Caspian—and dragged it on rolling logs to a river, maybe the Volga. When they got into a northern ocean, their talking oak branch warned them not to land on an island they came to, its magic was too strong, too deadly. That was Britain, or so Charles

Kingsley thought when he wrote his book of Greek hero tales."

Again Holly's eyes shone at him. Air thing he said, from the books he'd read to the thoughts he'd had, made her like him more.

"Their talking oak branch, in Greek folklore," she said. "Fraser's *Golden Bough* thinks the oak tree was worshiped everywhere, the way John said a moment ago. The Druids focused that belief, in old Britain."

"And here too," said Mr. Creed. "You and John make it sound like as if them Voths have got them their own sacred oak tree. The way you talk about it, it's a right big old tree."

"It's big, for a fact," I said. "You could cut it up into enough lumber to build you as big a house as this one. And you'd have planks left over to make a chicken coop."

"What was that term you used, Holly?" Luke inquired her. "The one for that sort of land where nothing was to be planted?"

"*Sith Bhruaith*, and that's more ancient Celtic," she told him. "The Goodman's Croft, but it isn't any good man it's set aside for."

"Like calling elves and trolls the Good People," said Luke, "because nobody dared call them bad. We have them here in these mountains, I think we're beginning to prove."

"Yes," said Holly, and she quoted:

> Up the airy mountain,
> Down the rushy glen,
> We daren't go a-hunting
> For fear of little men—

"Devil be damned to that!" snorted out Mr. Creed. "I ain't air been scared of little men nor yet either big ones.

What's them Voths think they're up to with me, first a-trying to scare me, then a-sending me all that sweet talk about neighborly doings? I got a mind to go up that there airy mountain you talk of, and do me some hunting."

His eyes were on his rack of guns, like as if he was a-getting ready to grab one of them and take off.

"Mr. Creed," said Holly, "I'm not at all sure that powder and lead would work against them."

"If lead won't work, silver will," said Mr. Creed. "I just so happen to have bullet molds, and I could run me some silver bullets. It wouldn't be the first time in these here parts a silver bullet found out a devilish witch-man."

Likely he was a-thinking of a case I knew, how Jack Bowdry had shot Kib Wordin with a silver bullet, and came clear in his murder trial when not one witness would speak up to swear Jack's life away. Mr. Creed was mad enough to shoot the same way his own self.

"I'll get word to them," he vowed, "tell them to come on down and fight me barehanded, both of them Voths at once. They've been a-using round Wolter Mountain long enough. Too damn long."

"Mr. Creed, they'd never dare fight you stand up, fair fight or two against one," I said. "Hark at Holly, and we'll make out how's the best way to beat them at their own game."

"No," said Luke suddenly, "not their own game. If you're fighting a wrestler, box him. And if he's a boxer, wrestle him."

"Maybe we should ought to have some of them Roman fellows youins been a-talking about," said Mr. Creed, quieted down a little bit. "You say they wiped out them Druids."

"And had their hands full doing it," said Luke. "From what little I gathered studying history, the Romans used plenty of their own magic charms to help themselves along. Probably they went in heavily for it, before invading the Isle of Man that time. I'm all for a little magic of our own."

His eyes were on Holly as he said it, but she shook her head.

"Just because you heard me read that prayer from Albertus Magnus, don't set me down as a magical expert," she said. "That's more in John's line."

"I'm not a magic-man either," I said. "I've seen things done, and been into them, but it was all American. These Voth brothers are from far off in that other land, and they've got things I don't know how to monkey with. Thank you kindly for the nomination, but I'd better not accept. I keep a-thinking of somebody else, if we can get him to help us."

"Who's that, John?" asked Luke.

"He's an old Indian chief and medicine man, lives only a few miles from here," I said. "Reuben Manco."

"That there old close-mouth?" said Mr. Creed. "I've been a-seeing him off and on for years, at Sky Notch. I've even traded him cabbage plants for tomato plants. But he sure enough does as little talking as he can manage. Round about three words a week. How come you to think he'd help, or could help if he would?"

"I met Reuben Manco at the state capital, in a bookstore where he was buying some Latin and Greek things," I said. "He loosened up with me a little tad. Other Indians allow he knows things from the old times that no other Indian knows. And I was at his place once, a-fetching him a message from a college professor. He was all right with me then."

"I don't even know where his place is," said Luke.

"If John knows, let's go bring him to talk these things over," Holly said.

"All right," said Mr. Creed. "If he'll come, he's welcome. He's Cherokee, I got it in mind."

"I'll do my best for the Cheyennes," said Holly.

"He's a Cherokee, all right," I said. "One of what they call the Civilized Tribes. They're a proud breed of Indian."

"So are the Cheyennes," she said.

Luke got up when she and I got up. "Can't I come too?" he asked, like a kid a-honing to be at a taffy break.

I felt for him, but I shook my head. "I'm not certain sure that Reuben Manco will even talk to me, Luke," I said. "Holly will be near about all the strangers for him to meet at first." I beckoned to her. "Come on, let's go over and try him."

Outside, it was different from inside. It was heavyish out there, like as if mist hung round us, though the sun shone. And it seemed to me I could hear a hum, the way you hear water a-falling down a rock, just round the bend of a trail out of sight. I couldn't be certain sure if it was a hum inside my head or outside. I said nothing to Holly, she said nothing to me. We got in her car and drove out of there.

The heaviness and the hum died off when we were out on the road, but still we said nothing. Not till I told her, "Just ahead, there to the right, you'll see two white rocks set. That's to mark Chief Reuben Manco's driveway in."

And she brought us there and turned off and drove up. A snaky, rocky driveway it was.

You couldn't see Reuben Manco's house from the road. The driveway curved up and then in through close-growing trees, a good climb of it, until you came to where the house was. It was built round, of poles driven into the dirt straight up and close together. Smaller poles were sort of braided in and out crossways, and outside all of that it was plastered in with clay and lime mixed, hard as cement and painted reddish brown. The roof was of flat walnut shakes, built to come to a point at the very top. The plank door hung on leather hinges. Rows of young beans and cabbages grew in front. Behind was parked his rattletrap old car.

Close in front of the door sat Reuben Manco himself, on a squarish chunk of rock, a-playing his old fiddle and a-playing it mighty well.

VI

He cut his deep-set eyes up at us when we got out of the car, but said nothing, didn't show he'd air seen me in his life. Reuben Manco wasn't much for being forward with visitors. He was small and wiry-made, and nobody knew for sure how old. Betwixt two hanging braids of lead-gray hair, his brown face was as hard and ready as the blade of a hatchet. He wore a tan shirt and tan pants, and beaded moccasins he'd likely made himself.

The bow stopped a-moving on the strings of the fiddle. Reuben Manco looked at us with those deep eyes as dark and bright as Holly's, and full of wisdom he mostly kept to himself.

"Good evening, Chief," I spoke up. "It's been a long piece of time since we've seen one another. You remember me—John."

"John," he recognized me, in a voice deep as a deep cave, the sort of voice Indians like to use when there's a stranger there. His eyes were on Holly.

"I've brought you a visitor," I said. "Let me make you known to Holly Christopher. She's a folklore lady and a true scholar, and one of the best friends I've got. I thought it would be good for you two to meet and be friends, too."

Reuben Manco put his fiddle down on his lap. "Scholar lady," his deep old voice repeated me. "Umh." He kept a-looking at Holly. "You been to school?"

"Out west, at Wichita State in Kansas," she said. "Then graduate work at the University of North Carolina at Chapel Hill. But I want to learn from other things than books."

"Other things," he boomed in his chest, solemn as a preacher in a church house. "What other things?"

"Things of nature," she said, and well I knew that she was trying her best with him. "Things about people—real people. Plants and animals. As much as I can see and hear and learn."

"Why you come here?" he asked her.

"Because John says you're strong in the wisdom of your people. That you know the truth of what was here before any white settlers came."

"That long ago?" he grunted. "Fool talk. I'm not that old."

"She's all right, Chief," I tried to speak for her, but he nair harked at me. He began to play the fiddle again, a whisper of old-time music. I sang with his tune:

Jinny went a-courting, Jinny went a-courting,
Jinny went a-courting with a smile;
You'd ought to been there when Jinny went a-courting,
You could hear her singing for half a mile . . .

He broke his music off and put his fiddle back on his lap again. "Why you come?" he asked her again. "Maybe come to laugh at old fool Indian."

It was like a charge in court.

"Chief, I'm Indian myself," she tried hard with him. "My grandmother was a Cheyenne, a *Tsi-tsi-chah*."

"Good tribe," he sort of growled. "I'm Cherokee. Different tribe."

"But I came to hear you speak, see what you do," she almost begged to him.

"Don't do anything," said Reuben Manco. "Just sit on this rock."

"Chief," she said, halfway like as if she was a-going to cry, "John would never have brought me here if he hadn't trusted me. I'm sorry if I've disturbed you. Maybe you wish we'd just go away, but—"

He laughed then, a small, short laugh. He grinned his fine old teeth, white as milk.

"All right, Miss Christopher," he said, not so deep now, nor either so growly. "Suppose we just drop this comic-book dialogue and hold ourselves a modest little seminar on comparative cultures. Call the way I acted an example of early American homespun humor. If you're Holly Christopher, I know your name from the *Journal of American Folklore*, your interesting article about certain parallel tales to the Tennessee Bell Witch."

She stared. "Oh, thank you," she breathed out. "You read the *Journal?*"

"Regularly," smiled Reuben Manco. "Now and then I contribute to it myself."

"Do you?" whispered Holly, and all of a quick sudden she sat down on the ground beside his rock, and tucked her feet under her. Right well she knew how graceful she looked that-a-way. He smiled, stroking the fiddle in his lap.

"It's a pleasure to welcome a true scholar of the Cheyenne blood," he said. "Not that I begrudge John's coming. Probably he has a strain of Indian heritage in him, at that. Most Americans do if their family has been around for seven or eight generations."

I squatted on my heels with my back to a tree and harked while Holly and Reuben Manco told one another about where they'd been to college and what professors they knew and what books they'd read. He'd graduated from Dartmouth up north, long years back, but he'd kept in touch with folks there, and Holly knew some of them.

All Holly had to say about the Voths, he heard and nodded as if he checked things over, likewise with what she told of the Gibb family. He took it in with a brown face chuck full of wisdom and maybe just a tad of worry.

"Druids," he repeated after her. "As you say, there's a whole cargo of notions about the Druids, mostly not worth consideration. But I've studied the few valid accounts of them from time to time, and so, I can see, have you."

"Not as much as I should have, I'm afraid," said Holly. "When you consider what we're up against here."

"We're up against more than just Druidism," said Reuben Manco, and, that's right, he said *we*, not *you*. "I agree that parts of their belief and practice can be evil. Dangerously evil. But twice as evil here," he said suddenly. "Where it might well mix into, crossbreed as you might say, with something else that's both similar and different."

"You all are five or six jumps ahead of me, Chief," I made bold to speak up. "I purely hate to butt in, a-seeing I don't have the schooling you and Holly got—"

"All right now, John, don't fish in shallow waters," he laughed at me. "You've told me in the past that your formal education is sketchy, but here and there, in various places, you've taken in considerable knowledge and training."

"I agree," said Holly. "John's a man of ripe sense and high native wit."

"Maybe not quite as native as with us Indians," said Reuben Manco, "but we need him in this problem." He turned his tone weighty again. "I'd suggest that some of the things John has seen and faced and handled—things that most people wouldn't believe, because nothing of the sort ever happened to them—have given him a unique strength in coping with evil. And, my young friends, evil is here in the neighborhood with us in carload lots, and it needs coping with in a high degree."

He questioned me, and I told about the big oak tree in front of the Voth house and what I'd glimpsed, or thought I'd glimpsed, up high in the shadow of its branches. And Holly mentioned what she'd read in that book, about the Man in the Oak.

"I don't doubt that he's there," said Reuben Manco. "I'm no more certain than you are what Reginald Scot meant by that term, but I wonder if I can't give you the name of this man in this oak." He crumbled a leaf of tobacco into the bowl of an old stone pipe. "How do you think that Gibb would suit?"

"Gibb?" said Holly after him. "Jonathan Gibb?"

"Not the Gibb who died here lately," said Reuben Manco, striking a match. "Another Gibb, first of the name who settled there. The story has come down with my people. He was able to take that particular tract without any protest from the Cherokee who lived nearby, because they themselves didn't even hunt there. It was bad medicine, if you'll permit me to use the Indian term." He puffed smoke. "No Cherokee had gone there in lifetimes."

"What was the trouble?" I inquired him.

"The Other-People who'd been there before and kept their gods there before the Indians," he said, smoking. "That stone figure you saw on the slope—once, long ago, our wise men thought it ought to be pulled apart and dragged down away. More than twenty strong braves hitched hide ropes to one of the stones and dragged and dragged—could barely move it a few feet. So goes the legend. Then there was a terrible wind, blowing down pine trees and rattling boulders like gravel. The braves felt less brave, and dragged the stone back. It took only half of them to hoist it uphill, when all of them had had trouble moving it downhill. Once it was in place again, the storm died down. That's why it was left alone by the Cherokee. Maybe that's why it's been left alone by white men."

"You make me shiver," said Holly, a-suiting the action to the word. "What has this to do with the Man in the Oak?"

"It has a connection," said Reuben Manco. "I was talking about the first Gibb to build there. He died in a strange way, I'm not sure how. But for some reason—had he committed suicide, I wonder?—he was buried in his own front yard, with a stake cut from an oak sapling driven through his heart."

"That's the way to hold down a vampire," Holly said.

"Whatever the reason for it," went on Reuben Manco, "that oak stake lived and grew and put out leaves and branches. It grew and grew. It got to be that big oak tree you saw there, two centuries old by now. And, when I listened to what John said about something scrambling in the shade of its leaves, I wondered if the stake really held down what it was supposed to hold. I wonder if it isn't the founder of the Gibb family, hanging in those branches like some kind of ape or bat, for whatever reason he may have to hang there."

We sat for a moment, chewing that much over. Reuben Manco studied Holly. "That charm you wear, like an elephant," he said. "What is it?"

"A Cheyenne medicine man gave it to me, but it came from some other tribe in the southwest. They knew about elephants."

"So did the old, old Cherokees. Gilushti, the Strong Hairy One—the ancient mammoth. It meant wisdom and power and charm against evil."

"Chief," I said, "how do you figure them a-trying to fence in Mr. Creed Forshay's rocky patch and then a-pulling up stakes when he made war medicine about it?"

"I hazard that they suspected he'd make the dispute public," said Reuben Manco. "I suggest that, the less public their possible wish for that rocky patch, the better for them."

"Why do they want it?" Holly asked. "Mr. Creed himself says, it's nothing to try to grow a crop on."

"Maybe the crop's already there," Reuben Manco said, puffing smoke. "Maybe already planted, long ago, and about to come to fruit, in a sort of unpleasant, crossbred way."

"In other words," said Holly, "they've brought one race of devils here to join forces with another."

"Well put," nodded Reuben Manco, drawing on his pipe. "You phrase things well. Because when you defeat a god, conquer him, he has to become a devil."

"Has to, Chief?" I said after him. "How do you figure?"

"By history, John, and a few guesses on prehistory. When a people was conquered, put under the yoke and heel of the conqueror, that people's gods were crushed and humbled. Nor matter if they'd been prayed to and thanked for the sun and the rain, for good times and for life after death."

I understood that.

"Those gods were flung out of their temples to make place for the gods of the victors," he went ahead. "Their images were smashed up and smeared with filth, they were laughed at and flouted and called false gods."

"False gods," said Holly after him.

"Nothing sounds falser than a false god," I said.

"Exactly," said Reuben Manco. "They were never

called gods again, except with false along with it. It was like that at the Roman conquest of Britain, the Moslem conquest of Persia and Syria and North Africa and Spain, the Spanish conquest of Mexico. False god became one word, like Damyankee with unreconstructed old Confederates. When Milton marshalled the hosts of Satan in hell, he called the roll of false gods." He smiled at Holly and smiled at me, with lips as hard as the sole of my shoe. "Very well, young friends, can you truly blame a broken, beaten god for becoming an outlaw, with an outlaw's motives and behaviors? For making a virtue of necessity and trying to fight back?"

"I see what you mean, Chief," I said, "but likewise I see what the thing means to me. Blame or not, we've got these things to fight, whether they're devils or gods. My saying is, throw punches at whatever the target might could be."

"Bravo!" cried Holly, and Reuben Manco smiled broader at her.

"It's always good to talk to John," he said. "He and I have the same thought about the problem, but he knows how to put things into words."

"I'm still trying to follow all this reasoning, Chief," said Holly.

"I follow it, some little bitty bit," I said. "What you're a-getting at is this, the way two things can join up into something bigger and get to be worse than either one of them. What's a-going on here is an old, old place of bad magic from those folks before the Indians, and then the Voth brothers fetched in their Druid things. So it's a mixtry betwixt the two."

Reuben Manco slitted his eyes at me. "Miss Christopher," he said, "I'll repeat myself here. John has found

69

out things in the life he's led that he might never have learned or dreamed of either at your university or mine. It's possible that he's been better off, being in charge of his own education."

"I'll endorse that viewpoint," she agreed. "What he says clarifies what you say."

"What he clarifies is an example of what has happened in other areas," said Reuben Manco. "Something coming from an old country to a new one can turn baleful there. Look at English sparrows, imported here as a sentimental gesture, and turning into a plague. Look at the problem the kudzu vine became when it was brought over from Japan."

"Or in Australia," Holly added on. "A settler brought a pair of rabbits with him. They and their progeny almost laid the whole continent waste."

"So, I suggest, with ancient old-world Druidism being joined to beliefs we used to have here. Religions do that, too. There was the Smoholla belief by Indians using their old legends along with Christianity, and it wound up in war. The same thing—bloodshed over religion—on what's called the Ghost Dance War."

"The massacre at Wounded Knee," said Holly, unhappy to say the name. "Horrible."

"That's the word for what happened, yes," Reuben Manco agreed her, "but who knows what would have happened if that massacre hadn't stopped it? Maybe Wovoka's prophecy would have come true; the white man and his works might have been swept away and the buffalo herds might have been born again."

"What you're a-getting at," I guessed, "is that the old-country Druid spirits are a-nudging those forgotten gods on Wolter, a-waking them up."

"Yes," nodding Reuben Manco, bending to put his

fiddle in its case. "Waking them up. And that, if you'll allow me to employ a bit of slang, will be Katy bar the door."

"Bar the door," I repeated after him. "It might could be hard to do, barring the door against such old gods."

Reuben Manco stood up off the rock. He stood up, not big, but straight and not old-looking the least bit. We two stood up with him.

"All this is rational discussion," he said, "but discussion, as John wants to say, isn't action. What are we going to do about all this?"

"That means you'll help us," said Holly gladly.

"If I can."

"Then come with us to Mr. Creed Forshay's and keep on a-talking." I made the bid to him. "Mr. Creed said for us to fetch you."

"I know Creed Forshay slightly," said Reuben Manco.

"And don't forget your fiddle," said Holly. "I love to hear you play."

He went into his cabin and came out again, carrying two glass fruit jars of something. "If I'm to visit there, I'll contribute my share to supper tonight."

He gave them to me to hold, and stopped for his fiddle case. I saw another thing he was a-bringing. Stuck in his belt behind was a hatchet, I reckon you'd call it a tomahawk. All of us got into Holly's car and we drove back to the Forshay place.

The sun was maybe an hour so above the mountain ridges when we got there. Mr. Creed shook hands with Reuben Manco, and to me they looked right wise and strong together. Luke was so glad to see Holly back, he stretched a grin near about all the way round his head. And I saw Holly smile back at him, the kind of smile a good man likes to get from a good woman.

"Proud to have you here, Chief," said Mr. Creed. "And right glad you'll help with what's got to be headed off from here."

"A job perhaps overdue, Mr. Forshay," said Reuben Manco.

In the house, he gave us a look at the two glass jars he'd brought. "That's stewed venison," he said. "I put it up last winter when I killed a white-tailed buck. You see it's jellied; I boiled the meat with the bones for that. And I seasoned it as it cooked, to make it tangy."

"What seasoning, Chief?" Holly wanted to know.

"Bay leaf mostly," he said. "And some tart pickle spices."

"And vinegar?"

"No," he grinned, "just some good blockade. It turns out more or less like a sort of wild-game sauerbraten in aspic. I consider it better cold than hot."

"We'll have some wild sallet greens with it," said Mr. Creed, near about to smack his lips. "Luke and I picked them here and yonder, while we waited for youins."

"I'll cook those," Holly spoke up, "very lightly, with a little green onion in them."

Luke beamed at her while she fixed the greens. We sat down to eat together. The jellied deer meat Reuben Manco had fetched along was mighty good, mighty good. Holly wanted to know the recipe, and Reuben Manco told it to her for her to write down. "You never can tell when I might come upon some good venison," she said. "I want to be ready for anything."

"Ready for anything," Reuben Manco repeated her. "All of us had better be ready for anything." He looked at me. "I feel better with you here, John."

"Thank you," I said. "I do my best most times, but I'm wondered if I know enough for this business. I still feel like as if I missed out on not going to a college somewhere."

"We all miss out on something, no matter what we do," said Mr. Creed. "I sit round harking at the things Luke learned himself at college, but I'm more proud than jealous over it."

"Just having a college degree doesn't give anybody a true intellectual superiority," said Holly, "though sometimes it takes intellectual superiority away." She looked sidelong at Luke. "I don't mean you," she said.

"I know, Holly," said Luke.

Mr. Creed allowed that, like Holly and me, he was wondered why the Voths had those strong feelings about the rocky patch they'd tried to fence off. Reuben Manco said he'd been giving the thing some thought of his own.

"I've been trying to remember everything I can about it," he said to us. "I have only old, old legends to go on, things that have been passed on from one generation to another. Mind you, I didn't see this thing I'm going to tell about. Neither did any of the Indians who were in this Wolter Mountain country when the first of the white settlers came." He fixed Holly with his black eyes. "It may have been thousands of years ago," he said, "and it was told by the old Cherokees to the young ones, all through those centuries, those thousands of years."

"And we're a-waiting to hear it today, Chief," said Mr. Creed.

"They say there was war, far back in those times," said Reuben Manco, his voice going deep, like as if he was a-making a speech. "The Indians fought the ancient Other-People who were here first. They say that the Indians were better with bows and spears and hatchets, but that the Other-People were better with magic spells. The magic of the Other-People confused Indians making an attack or lying in wait by a trail. Most of all, that magic was strongest at the foot of the worship-place of the Other-People, the very place where today you see that figure laid out in heavy stones, with that plot of ground full of rocks at its feet."

"I nair heard aught of this," confessed Mr. Creed.

"How could you hear it?" Reuben Manco's deep voice asked him. "Not even all the Indians know about it today. But it's my business to know it—I'm a medicine man. I must keep the old stories, the old wisdoms." And he bit into a piece of corn bread and drank some coffee.

"Well, about the rocky patch," I said, "I've been there three times these last two days. The first time, I noticed what looked faces, or like maybe the shadows of faces, on the rocks. The second time, they came out plainer. The third time, plainer still, pure down a-looking at me. It wasn't just because I'd seen them the other two times, because they were plain to Holly."

"Very plain," Holly agreed me. "I could believe they lived once."

"Your old Druids, pagan Celts, believed that in England and in old Gaul," said Reuben Manco. "When they made stone images, those images were thought to live. To be thinking, living creatures that drank the blood spilled for them."

I felt chilly about that. I reckon we all did.

"Only," went on Reuben Manco, "what I told you was long before the Druids in England. It concerns the Other-People who ruled here before my people."

"Chief," said Holly, "if this goes into speculations about visitors from across space, I have to say that I don't believe in such things, not yet. I'm waiting to be convinced."

"Like the things in Genesis," said Mr. Creed. "Abraham

entertaining them angels unawares, and the other angel that wrestled all night with Jacob and then blessed him. Gave him that long life and all them sons of his that each of them was father of a tribe of the Jews."

"You've read the book of Genesis, Mr. Creed," said Reuben Manco. "Studied it."

"I study all the Bible," said Mr. Creed. "I've done read it through time and again. I can quote you chunks of it from memory."

"I hark back one more time to something Holly talked about," said Luke. "How men, or something like men, might have been in America as much as a quarter of a million years ago. Might have been ancient before Chief Manco's first fathers came over Bering Strait from Asia."

"Such things might could fetch out the tales that keep a-bobbing up here and yonder amongst these hollows and ridges," I said. "Like things about death-devils and such."

"The Raven Mockers," said Reuben Manco. "The bringers of death."

"Is that a Cherokee belief?" asked Holly. "I don't know it."

"It's the rumor of the spirits, or wild strange beings, that gather to make somebody die," said Reuben Manco. "The Raven Mockers—I don't know exactly why they're called that—close in on a man. Close his eyes and quench his breath, as Alan Seeger says in his poem. Maybe they kill him, maybe he gets away somehow. They fly or flutter, the old men told me when I was young. They have arms to use like wings, or wings to use like arms. Nobody really sees them to live and tell about them. But when death is near, you can hear the flap of their arm-wings."

I told myself not be believe I heard a flapping sound outside, like a shirt in a high wind.

"Well, I've finished eating a good dinner," said Reuben

Manco, like somebody a-finding something else to talk about.

He got up and went to open his fiddle case. Beside the case lay the hatchet he'd fetched in his belt. He saw me looking.

"That's nicely made," I said to him. "It was hammered out by hand, not stamped out by factory machinery. Who did it?"

"I did," he said, fiddle in hand. "It's a medicine hatchet."

I noticed a feather tied to the end of the handle.

"Before we get into what we have to do," he said, "I suggest we have some music. You white Americans say the devil is afraid of music."

"That's what I hear tell once in a while," said Mr. Creed. "Maybe music can set the devil back from our door. One old saying goes that if you're not in the devil's power more than seven times a day, you're a-doing all right."

"That was said by Alexandre Dumas," Luke told us, a-giving a Frenchy sound to the name.

"I think some people are in the devil's power just once a day," said Reuben Manco, bending his ear to listen to how he tuned his fiddle. "Just once a day, all day, three hundred and sixty-five days a year. What shall we play, gentlemen?"

Luke and I had brought out our instruments and we got the tunings right all round. We did a verse or so of the Blockader song:

> I been a blockader for thirty long years,
> I spent all my money for whiskey and beer,
> I'll go to the valley and set up my still
> And I'll run you a gallon for a two-dollar bill . . .

"Good blockade comes another sight higher than that these days," said Mr. Creed, a-humming it. "But shouldn't we ought to have some sacred hymn if we're a-going up against the devil?"

We did "Mary she heard a knock in the night." Holly knew that one and sang sweetly with the tune:

> Mary she heard a knock in the night
> And she turned her key of gold
> To open her cabin door, and then
> She seen three great big beardy men
> A-standing out in the cold.

> O Lady Mary, the first man said,
> O let us come in at your door,
> For to see that baby upon your breast.
> We've traveled our way from the east to the west
> A thousand miles and more . . .

Mr. Creed joined in with Holly. He had a deep, tuney bass voice. "I sure enough do love that song," he said.

Reuben Manco set down his fiddle at last and got up and went to look out the door. "Full moonlight," he said, "and it so happens that this is Midsummer Eve."

"A special festival of the Druids," Holly said softly.

Luke frowned. "This is the twenty-third day of June," he said. "I thought Midsummer Day was the twenty-first."

"No," said Reuben Manco, "that's the summer solstice, the longest day of the year. The twenty-fourth is the first day when there's a noticeable change in the length of the sun's stay in the sky, somewhat the way Christmas comes just after the winter solstice. And if our friends the Voths are at all correct in their Druidical rituals, they'll be doubly glad to have a full moon tonight." He came back from the door. "They just might be out in this bright night, getting their nerve up to pay a neighborly visit."

"That's a fact, and I've got a notion about it," said Mr. Creed, getting up, too. "Holly would do well to come and sleep in the house tonight."

"She can have my room," said Luke, right away quick. "I'll hustle my stuff out, and if Chief Manco is going to stay here, he and I can make up pallets on this floor."

"Come on, Holly," said Mr. Creed, taking a lantern off a hook. "I'll go out yonder with you and stand by while you get whatever you want to bring in here."

He and she went out together. Reuben Manco stood at the door, a-watching them and a-watching the blaze of the moon. He hummed another verse of what we'd played about Lady Mary and the Three Wise Men.

Luke walked close to where I sat. "John," he said, a-leaning close so I could hear his whisper, "I let Papa go and fetch in Holly's stuff, because I've got to talk to somebody, about Holly and me."

"Why not talk to Holly?" I inquired him.

"Well, I'm beefing up my courage to do that. John, I never saw or heard of a girl like that. I've had dates here and there with various girls, but I never felt anything serious. But Holly—God in heaven, John, if she'd only look my way."

"I've seen her look your way," I said to him. "I think she looks your way a right much of the time. And she's remarked to me about how good a fellow you shape up to be."

"Has she?" he half squeaked, he was so glad to hear that word. "You think she feels like that toward me?"

I had to smile. "All I'm a-telling you is how it seems to

me, a-watching from the sidelines. My unasked advice is, take up the subject with her."

Right then, we heard a wild, wild scream outside, a woman's scream, the voice of Holly, loud and scared halfway to death.

VII

Which of us jumped up first, I can't now rightly say for certain. What I do know is that, while the scream still flickered in the air, all three of us jammed and wiggled to get out the front door together. Outside, I was the fastest on my feet a-running for the stable, with Luke Forshay and Reuben Manco together, just a hop behind me.

In the bright moonglow in front of the stable door, Mr. Creed lay on the ground, quiet as a rock. Beside him was flung the lantern, busted and gone out. I dropped down on one knee alongside of him.

"Holly!" yelled out Luke. He ran on past me into the stable. "Holly!"

Reuben Manco stopped beside where I knelt. "Leave him alone, John, unless you know how to handle a concussion case." He squatted on his moccasin heels and felt all over Mr. Creed's head with the tips of his fingers. He acted like a man who knows what he's up to.

Luke came out of the stable again, on a sail of a run. He carried Holly's suitcase and dropped it next to us.

"This was in there, at the foot of the ladder," he yammered. "She's gone, she's been carried away—" He headed off amongst the trees. "Holly!" we could hear him call.

Reuben Manco still worked his hands over Mr. Creed's head. "There's no fracture, as well as I can judge," he said to me. "Thank whatever gods there may be for that. And no open scalp wound. He must have been hit with something soft and heavy, perhaps a sandbag."

"Holly!" we could hear Luke again, farther off among the night trees.

Reuben Manco put his hand flat on Mr. Creed's chest. "He's breathing heavily," he reported. "Ah," he said, for Mr. Creed made out to stir.

"Devil be damned," said Mr. Creed, barely a whisper of it.

"Now he seems to be coming out of it," allowed Reuben Manco.

"Seven," Mr. Creed mumbled, loud enough this time to be heard well. "Seven, they told me."

He tried to sit up. I saw that his hands were clenched.

"Let's get him to the house, John," said Reuben Manco, cool as a mountain spring. "Be careful with him, though. If he can move a little, that should help him come out of it. But don't let him make too much of an effort at first."

We hoisted Mr. Creed up on his feet betwixt us. Each of us got an arm of his and dragged it over our necks. As we started for the house, he grunted and started to move his feet to walk. "Hold him up," said Reuben Manco, and we half dragged, half toted him along, step after step. In the front room we lowered him into his armchair.

He sagged with his head down, like somebody a-having a snooze over the newspaper. He kept his big, corded hands fisted tight shut. "Seven," he said, one more time. "Seven in the way."

I held him up in the chair while Reuben Manco got ice from the refrigerator and put it into a towel and jammed it against the back of Mr. Creed's neck. With a wet cloth in the other hand, he carefully mopped and wiped Mr. Creed's face. Mr. Creed blinked and snorted, and again he tried to get up on his feet.

"Let me have a drink," he grumbled. "There's some yonder in—"

"No whiskey just yet," said Reuben Manco, like somebody who had a right to give the orders. "Is there any coffee in the pot on the stove, John?"

I looked into the pot. "Yes, there's some, but it's near about cold."

"Pour him a cup of it and get the rest hot."

I fetched the cup and Reuben Manco took it and held it for Mr. Creed to drink from, while I went back to get the fire started. Mr. Creed blew out his breath. At last his fists came open. Something fell out of one of them, on the floor. I picked it up and knew what it was. The elephant thing that Holly had worn round her throat.

Reuben Manco kept on a-working the ice pack behind Mr. Creed's neck. "You're coherent, Mr. Forshay," he said. "That's a very good sign. Talk to us if you can, it will help clear your head for you."

"They jumped me up from behind," Mr. Creed made out to say. "They grabbed that Holly girl, and I grabbed her back from them, and when I tried to fight them, one of them hit me over the head and knocked me flat as a pancake. I heard what they was a-saying." His voice rose, harsh and fierce. "Seven, they said, seven in the way!"

"Seven what?" I inquired him.

"Seven in the way," he repeated himself.

"A warning, I'd judge," said Reuben Manco, busy with the ice and the cloth.

"There was five or six of them against me," said Mr. Creed.

"Did you know them?" Reuben Manco asked.

"Couldn't see them for no good. They looked black, is all I can swear myself to. And floppy."

"Did they have robes on?" Reuben Manco asked him. "Hoods? Masks?"

"Maybe so, I can't tell you."

"Give him more coffee if it's hot, John," Reuben Manco told me. "All right, Mr. Creed, you're sitting up better, you're becoming articulate. No complications, we can hope, from that blow on your head; but stay quiet."

"It hurts like hell, and I can still see sparks," said Mr. Creed. "Hey, where's Luke at?"

"He's gone after Holly," I said. "He went while we were a-looking after you."

"They'll get Luke, too!" he blared out and shuffled his feet to get up, but Reuben Manco shoved him back into the chair.

"You'll stay right where you are until you're better," Reuben Manco gave him the order. "We'll go find Luke in a moment. But first, answer me some questions." He looked hard into Mr. Creed's eyes. "Do you see me clearly?"

Mr. Creed glowered up at him. "Sure enough I do, right clear."

"What was your father's full name?"

"Anson Trevis Forshay. What's he got to do with all this?"

"We can say that there's no brain damage," allowed Reuben Manco, happy to say it. "You'll be back to normal pretty soon. But I tell you to stay quiet, I don't want you blanking out on us." He turned around to me. "I said to bring him some more coffee."

I poured it out and Reuben Manco held it for Mr. Creed to drink of it. Then Mr. Creed allowed he felt better, only his head ached like a bad tooth and he was plumb wrought up about Luke. "Could they might be a-killing him?" he said.

"No, hardly anything like that," said Reuben Manco, in so sure a voice that it made me feel sure, too. "Whoever or whatever came out here tonight with just a sandbag didn't mean to kill, or probably you'd be dead yourself. They may capture Luke, but if they did we'll get him back. What are you up to there, John?"

I'd taken time to look at that elephant charm. I tied the broken string back together and slung it round my neck.

"Go on, keep talking," Reuben Manco said to Mr. Creed. "How did you happen to have that amulet in your hand?"

"It was when Holly screamed out," said Mr. Creed. "I was out at the door, I seen things a-coming, just black things I couldn't make out clear, the way I told you. I grabbed a hold on her to pull her round and put myself in front of her, and I reckon the thing come a-loose then. Next second, I got clubbed and knocked out. Now she's out yonder somewheres, and Luke too, and what is it that's got them?" His voice rose up on that.

"I'll go find out about it," I said, swiveling round with my face to the door.

"And I'll come along with you," vowed Reuben Manco. "We'll start the moment Mr. Creed here promises he'll stay quiet until we get back."

"All right, all right, I promise," Mr. Creed near about snarled at him. "But get them back safe, you hear? Better take you some guns."

"Guns aren't all that much good most nights, especially with what I suspect we may be running into," said Reuben Manco. "I've got this," and he patted his belt to make sure of his tomahawk. "John, I see you've got a good knife in that sheath. Yes, and that powerful charm on your neck."

"When in the name of everything that's hellacious are

youins a-going to start after them?" barked out Mr. Creed.

"We'll go right now." Reuben Manco moved past me to the door and looked back with his hand on the knob. "You sit right where you are, however hard it is to do that. Concentrate on feeling better. And trust us. We'll fetch back both those young people to you. That's the word of a chief."

"Thanks for a-saying it that-a-way," said Mr. Creed, softer in his voice. "Chief," he added on.

"Come on, John."

Reuben Manco and I went out together. It was the kind of night where the full moon poured itself down, seemed for a moment to be near about as bright as the sun. The open patches were pale with the light. But under the trees lay shadows like puddles of black water. The moon couldn't soften them like the sun. For the sun lives; and the face of the moon is only the ghost face of Earth's dead child, a-looking down, maybe a-trying to say it would come back home if it could.

Reuben Manco went to where some stakes and poles leaned up against a big pile of sawed logs. He picked up one, put it down, and chose him another. That one looked to be from a locust tree, near about seven feet long and sharpened to a point at one end, maybe to drive into the ground for a stake. He weighed the balance of it in his hand. I started off for the path by the fish pond.

"We don't go that way, John." He came up alongside me with the pole in his hand. "No sense in trying the regular trail up. Didn't Mr. Creed Forshay say something about seven in the way?"

"What other way is there?"

"Come along with me." He turned and headed off under some oak branches. "Back this way is a climb I

85

remember from when I was just a boy, prowling here without asking the leave of Mr. Forshay's father before him." He used his pole to feel for good footing. "Come along with me," he said again.

I did that thing. I've learned to move at night, even now and then during the war times when you had to do it without noise or a-stumbling if you wanted to live through the walk you took. Reuben Manco took us to where a little stream whooshed along to go to the fish pond. It was only a long step across it, though when I made the step I wondered if something I saw down in the water might could be a snake out for a moonlight swim. On the yonder side, we went up a slope amongst trees, along the rows of the good garden the Forshays kept. Beyond that was the big earthenware tile set up over a stone-and-cement basin to filter the water that came down from the spring on Wolter Mountain and flowed to the house. Reuben Manco pointed off with his stick.

"This way," he told me, "but I doubt if there's any sort of path, so stay close behind me and step where I step."

There were thick-growing laurels there, and I couldn't exactly hear into them, but I had the feeling that something was on the move there, under the cover of the laurels, right along beside us. I didn't say aught about it, though. I just kept on my way after Reuben Manco.

It was right dark for a while there, for Wolter Mountain loomed up over us. Reuben Manco kept on ahead, almost like as if he could see. I wondered myself if he'd been born at midnight, the way old folks say a child born that-a-way can find his way in the dark. We went on for maybe twenty minutes, as I judged. Beyond then, I saw light, where the mountain must be chopped open for the moon to come through.

"I remember this place," said Reuben Manco, heading for where that good light soaked in.

And I followed. And meanwhile, the thing I felt without rightly a-hearing it, seemed to come a-moving in the laurels to keep us company.

We worked our way through heavy scrub for quite some distance, it might could be half a mile. Then we came out into a cleared space amongst the trees, and I could look up a rough, rugged, knobby old wall of rock, I didn't know how high. At the top of it, the round moon hung and looked down, maybe a-wondering what in the name of gracious we were up to.

"When we get up there," said Reuben Manco, like as if we were there already, "it won't be so steep on top, the two or three miles we'll have left to travel to where you say the Voth cabin is."

"We're a-going to climb up yonder in the night?" I wondered him.

"We have the light of a full moon," he replied me. "It may be promoting a Druidical sacrifice when it gets to the top of the sky, but not before then. Just now, it will show us our way up."

The pale moonlight seemed to agree him. It poured itself on that set of high, steep rocks that went up not quite as straight as the side of a house. I stood in a mess of some sort of weeds that crackled under my shoes. I looked up the mountain, but then again I heard something, and looked that-a-way to see.

The noise came from a hobby of laurel scrub all grown close and tangled enough to be like the weaving of a basket. It was a noise that rattled and grumbled at the same time, like something that pushed through and breathed hard as it pushed. Something alive. I swung myself the rest of the way round to have a clear look, and then what I saw made me just stand still amongst crackly weeds, stand like as if I'd taken root with them.

A big, lumpy darkness wallowed itself out from under

the laurel leaves. It stopped halfway into the open, with the moon on the front of it, so that I could plainly make it out.

A pig, a boar pig. And no ordinary runaway from some farmer's hog lot. You nair got to see a boar pig like this one, not much often in the time of your life. Nor either would you care to.

At that first look, it was a white-tusked boar pig, near about a size to pull a wagon. Later on, I was able to judge it might could weigh four hundred pounds, enough to butcher out for a whole precinct barbecue. But just then at that moment, it only looked big, big, and mean, mean.

Its head was the biggest, meanest part to it, I thought as I stood still and looked. A huge, meaty old head that sloped back onto shoulders that were big, too, but looking less than that head. It had chunky, slaty-shaggy jowls, and shoe-sized ears hiked up to hark at things, and eyes like two chunks of feldspar a-glinting, and a wet, slick nose that wobbled up and down. It had tusks, pale white as fresh milk in a moonbeam that struck them, tusks the size of meat hooks in a butcher shop, a-sprouting out of its jaw to right and left and curled up to points sharp enough for hunting knives. The glinty eyes blinked and gopped, a-trying to make out for sure what it saw in the bright night. The whole thing was dark and swolled out as bristly as a bear, but with a frosted, speckly shine to the bristles. Gentlemen, that boar pig looked dangerous.

I stood right there where I was, still as a stone, a-doing my best not to crackle those weeds at my feet. A tad of breeze blew toward me from that boar pig, so I knew it couldn't rightly whiff my scent. I hoped it might could miss the sight of me if I didn't make a move. But it saw me all right. I heard it bubble its breath out, like as if it had smacked its big slobby mouth. And then, out it came at me, with a sort of scrambling run.

I could swear that I saw its hoofs strike fire out of a rock, like as if they'd been shod with iron. My quick thought was, let it get almost to me and at the last moment jump out to the side. Maybe it would just charge past. That wouldn't be much of a chance to get away, but right then I could think of naught else to do.

Out of that laurel thicket it slammed its big, shaggy self and toward me. That was when Reuben Manco made his own charge, from the left side of it as it came.

He shoved at it with the sharpened point of his locust pole. He leaned into that pole as it tore into the hairy side. I saw him plant his moccasined feet, dig down to get all his weight into the shove, the stab. His back hiked itself up like an old tomcat a-going into battle. He rammed his pole in and in and into that boar pig's flank, so hard it stumbled away in front of him.

I heard a hurt scream go up, loud and wild, the sort of sound you'd hear if somebody took the lid off of hell.

That big, rushing body went over and down in a scramble of hoofs, smacked down on its side. Then it turned over on its back, all the way over, a-rolling as it went. It yelled out again in the pain it felt. I saw all four of those sharp hoofs as they raked up in the moony air. It had gone down so close to me, a big spurt of blood splashed out on my shoes as I jumped away like a scared grasshopper.

Reuben Manco stood back off from it, a-watching. I walked toward him, and I don't take no shame whatever when I say that my knees hit one against the other.

"Luckily I was on the side where the heart was," said Reuben Manco, as quiet and cheerful as if we'd been out a-gigging for frogs.

The big boar pig still quivered himself, but he was done for. Reuben Manco had put that pointed locust pole into him like a spear, so hard it came clean out on the other side. Blood flowed from where it was stuck, shiny black in the moonlight. Reuben Manco turned on his heel and looked to where I'd been a-standing.

"Probably it was to our advantage that you were right where that chicory grows," he allowed, still in his calm Indian-chief way.

"Chicory?" I repeated him.

I looked, too. Sure enough that's what the crackly patch was. I saw the bare spikes of stems, the chubby little leaves, the flowers in the moon that, by sunlight, would have been pale blue. "Chicory?" I said again.

"I've heard old men say that it's a help against evil enchantment," Reuben Manco told me.

"Evil enchantment?" I repeated him again, and I knew how stupid I must sound.

Reuben Manco swung back round to look closer at the boar pig. It lay quiet now, except for a little quiver in its stubby legs.

"You see, this was never a tame boar," he said, still cool, still in charge of things, the way I'd begun to expect of him. "This one isn't really native in this part of the world at all."

"That's a true fact, Chief," I said, a-getting hold of myself at last. "I've seen such as that, one-two times here and there in these mountains."

And likewise I knew how came them to be wild in the wildest hollows and woodsy places. Early on in this century, some Englishmen bought themselves a mountain or two to make into a hunting ground, and over from the old country they shipped some wild boar pigs, sows too, to breed themselves up and give them some special sport. But then, along came the war—the first one to have the name of a world war, in 1914. All those English fellows went a-hastening back home to get into the fight. But the old-country wild boar stock was left behind. It bred up by itself and ranged round, high and low, a-raiding garden patches and a-killing dogs that got too close. Hunters had gone out to try to kill them off, and now and then a hunter had been killed off his own self. And right there before us lay one of the wild boar pig breed, stabbed through from one side to the other by Reuben Manco's sharp pole, put through it like a spear.

"Here's what I'm trying to rationalize," said Reuben Manco, and drew himself a deep breath to help his thinking. "The Druids held the boar in high, mystical respect. They thought it had powers of magic."

He took in another breath, as deep as a well.

"Remember, John," he lectured on, still as calm as somebody at the dinner table, "Mr. Creed Forshay said that the Voths, or whoever attacked him, promised something about seven in the way. Seven perils, I would suggest, against anybody who dared try to follow."

"You're right, he said that thing," I agreed him. "Seven in the way, that's what he allowed they said." Again I looked at the boar pig, a-lying on the ground, gone as quiet as a bag of old clothes. "And maybe this was the first of the seven."

"I agree with you, John," nodded Reuben Manco. "I want to hope so, at least. Because, if it was, that leaves only six more for us to face and deal with."

He turned his wiry old back on what he'd killed. He gazed off and up at that high, steep mountain.

"We'd better get on our way, while that light's at its best." He swiveled his wise, brown old face round to look at me. "Do you feel as if you could try it?"

Right at that time, with what we'd gone up against and seen whipped and killed, I sure enough felt I could try it.

"Come on, Chief," I said to him.

VIII

But, naturally, it wasn't that easy, nair bit.

I went along with Reuben Manco to the cliff. When we got next to it, I thought it looked another sight steeper up and down than it did from a little way yonder. I flung my head back on my neck and gazed up and up, and it put me in mind of once when I was in a big city and my friends had me to visit the tallest skyscraper they had.

Only, no windows there, the way you've got windows in a skyscraper. No cornices nor either windowsills. And, sure enough, no fire escape.

"Yes," Reuben Manco was a-saying. "I can make out the way we used to climb here, years ago. We started on these fallen rocks."

There was a clutter of them there, close up together, like a baby child's play-toy blocks in a tumble. Reuben Manco hopped up on one, hopped from that to a higher one and then to the highest of them. "Yes," he said to me again. "Come on up here and I'll show you."

I followed him, hop by hop. I had it in mind his moccasins were better for this kind of job than my big old clodhopper shoes. When I was side by side with him on that highest hunk of rock, he put his hand on the cliff face. Shadows hung there, in a jaggy, slanty line from up above.

"This crack is what we used when I was young," he told me. "You can see, it's deep and solid. Back in the times of the glaciers, it must have frozen and then broken open. And up above, you can see another one running across the cliff's face, about four feet up. The two of them make us a sort of double grip for both hands and feet. How strong are your hands and feet?"

"Right good for a mountain man, I'd say," I replied him.

"Yes, I've watched your hands on the guitar. Those fingers look as strong as the claws of a hammer. I'll start up now, I know the way. Give me a few feet the lead of you, then come along as I do. As we go up here, I'll tell you from time to time what to expect to find."

He set a moccasin toe in the lower crack, hoisted himself like a horseman a-using a stirrup, and got both hands clamped in that upper crack. Face to the cliff, he began to work his way along the slant. He sort of sneaked at it, like a lizard.

I couldn't hold back if I'd wanted to. Up I hiked my own foot and jammed it into the crack. I hoisted myself and grabbed the place above. It was inches deep, I figured, and I started to sidle along and up, after Reuben Manco. My nose was close to the stretch of rock we had to climb. Granite, I judged it. That meant that once there had been fire there, blasts of it that tore big mountains open and melted them down and then stopped so the mountains could cool again into new shapes. I had thoughts the like of that as I dragged myself along, a little small step at a time—move a foot ahead, reach a hand along, then the other hand, then bring up the other foot.

We kept a-slanting our way up. I reckon we did that sort of journey for two hundred and fifty feet or more, which took us up maybe for seventy-five. Finally Reuben Manco's quiet, cool voice bade me go slow as I got to where he'd stopped and was a-studying. I stole me a look toward where he was. He hung to the cracks and peered up.

"These seams come to an end at this point," he allowed. "Now, up there, we climb on a sort of natural ladder. You'll see that there are two kinds of stone here. Over a long space of time, the soft rock was washed away, and the hard pieces are left for us to take hold of."

When he'd said that, he reached above him and got a grip someway and started to climb on ahead, as steady as if he did it every moonlit night of his life.

I hunched along by those two cracks until I stood where he'd stood. He'd already made it up to about seven or eight feet above me. I could see those chunks of rock he'd mentioned. They stuck out of the cliff in little points and blobs and ledges. I laid hold on one and it seemed right solid. I could grab hard onto it. I reached higher to a one beyond that and drew a breath and started to swarve my way up. I got my toe into the upper crack and that helped me up to where I was a-following just below Reuben Manco.

Gentlemen, it was a hard go of it. He was long years older than I was, but he didn't weigh so much and he was as hard and limber as a braided rawhide whip. Likewise, as I reckoned, those moccasins he had on made better climbing things than my big, heavy shoes. Not that I took the time right then to envy him or the like of that. I pressed myself to the cliff, a-hanging on by my toes and fingers and maybe my eyelids, while I reached up a hand to grope for a rock chunk to bear my weight and then inched myself to it. That's how it felt, an inch at a time.

One thought I did have in my head as I scrambled and scraped my way up. It was the thing I used to hear old folks say about how you should profit by your mistakes. I told myself that if I made one mistake on this cliff, just one, I'd nair last long enough to figure the profit of it. And I grabbed on all the tighter to the next little ledge.

I knew I'd started to puff my breath, not much but some. My muscles felt good on me, shoulders, arms, legs. I'd kept in shape through the years. I've walked twenty miles in a day to visit choice friends, and at the end of that day I've danced at a frolic till near about sunup. I was glad I'd always moved round to keep strong and supple.

Just once I slipped, and it wasn't purely my fault. A knob I grabbed with my hand came loose out of the cliff, like an apple out of a barrel, and for one second I slipped away. But I grabbed on again, with a rock where I'd had firm hold below, and I hung there, getting my feet set on other places. Of all things, I thought back on a trick problem I'd had in school arithmetic, the one about the frog at the bottom of the well, that could climb up three feet and then slide back two. I used to feel for that poor old frog, with his climbing and sliding, and I felt glad for him that he got out of the well at last, with us scholars to figure how long it took him. If the frog could get out of the well, I reckoned, I should ought to get to the top of the cliff.

Then there came a stretch that was less like a wall and more like the pitch of a roof, and that was easier and not so nervish. The crawl upward on it was near about like a rest to my fingers, though the rock was hard and scrapy to my knees. Reuben Manco hung at the top of that slope where it got steep again. When I caught up to him, he showed me a winding crack, like a crooked chimney, that went up the steep new stretch. A-making the climb along there took doing, took thought. I kept on a-thinking, Reuben Manco knows what he's up to here, and he's enough well acquainted with me to figure I can do whatever he does. And the moon was on us, like as if its glow

washed us all over. Above the place where the crack pe-
tered out, we came again to just little bumps and juts to
hang onto and try to find more above them. In my time
I've heard tell of mountain climbers, with the one who
said he climbed up the highest mountain in the world just
because it was there. All right, this mountain was there,
and it had to be climbed. We climbed it.

Just when it began to appear to me like as if I'd been
on the scramble forever and ever, I heard Reuben Manco
from up there over my head, "All right, John, here we are
at the top."

Gentlemen, I was pure down glad to hear him speak
those words. I didn't look up, because that would have
meant a-hiking my head back, and I felt better with my
nose close to the rock that right there was right close to
straight up and down. I grabbed a few more rough
places, got my feet set where they could find their place,
and made way higher, made it higher. My face came up
over the rim of a ledge, and I could make out a broad
place almost flat, and higher up the moon's face, hung
there round and close. Reuben Manco was already on his
feet. He watched while I got a knee up and then the
other knee up and crawled on across the ledge and finally
stood up next to him.

And didn't it feel good to be a-standing there, with
what seemed to be soft ferns in a tumbly patch around
our feet and the moon a-flooding down its bath of light on
us after we'd finished our climb. I looked round to see just
where we'd come to. The ledge went on as wide as a cow
lot. On the far side, with the moon held from it, was a
black, tree-grown hump of Wolter Mountain, but nothing
like what we'd just put down under us. In that direction,
I figured, would be the way to the Voth place and whatever the Voths were up to there where they lived.

Reuben Manco fumbled a hand at the left side of his belt. He fetched it away with something in it. "Here John," he said, holding out an old army canteen. "Have some water."

I gopped at him. I'd nair noticed he had such a thing with him. I took the canteen and unscrewed the cap and poured water into my mouth. I didn't swallow it right down, I made it roll and wash over my tongue and back in my throat, so that it seeped into me by trickles. It felt fine. I handed him back the canteen.

"How come you to fetch that along?" I inquired him.

"Don't tell me you never noticed," he half-joked me. "Usually you notice everything. It's a habit of mine, when I go on an expedition through this country. I just hook it on my belt, the same way I do my tomahawk. It's apt to come in handy. But how do you feel, now you're up here?"

I opened and shut my two hands a time or two. My fingers felt achy, that was a fact, and they knew they'd been hard at work, but they were still strong. I rocked myself back and forth on my toes. I flexed my arm muscles, and I hiked my shoulders to get the cricks out.

"I reckon I'll do," I replied him. "I'm fair to middling. I feel like as if I'd been a-chopping weeds in a corn patch, but that will pass off directly, now we don't have to climb like that again, not right off."

I thought how good it felt to stand solid on that ferny stretch, with the moon for company to us. Reuben Manco mopped his brow with his sleeve and grinned to me, then he took a drink from the canteen himself.

"I doubt if we'll have to do another perpendicular climb like that one. Yes, it was difficult."

I breathed a deep one. "Maybe that was number two of the seven things they put in our way," I offered him.

"No," said Reuben Manco, seriously, "I hardly think that. Because the cliff was already there before any Druidical charms. It's been there since those beginnings of things we talked about earlier this evening. I suspect we still have six matters to face, carefully and skillfully prepared for us."

He capped the canteen and slid it back into its pouch and snapped the fastenings on it. He walked across through the ferns, toward another drop of the cliff. That one was in darkness, the moon didn't reach it. He studied a clump of brush a-growing close to the edge.

"I'm glad to find this," he allowed, and bent to tear off some twigs of it. I watched while he rubbed it between his hands and then rubbed his palms over his face.

"It's cedar," he said. "The smell of cedar is supposed to be a protection against ghosts and all evil spirits. My people used to burn its needles at their doorways to fend off any spell of ill magic."

"Is that a fact, Chief?" I said.

"It's what they used to do, and here and there still do," he replied me. "And they were wise about things like that. Here, let me pick some for you."

He went and stooped above another scrubby clump of cedar, right at the edge.

That was when the edge crumbled itself away and Reuben Manco went right down out of my sight, like as if a hand had come a-reaching up and snatched him off into nothing.

I could feel my eyes and my mouth stretch out wide. If the Voths could do the like of that to us, we were as good as done for, right then. "Chief!" I yelled out, alone in the moonlight night.

"Here," came up his voice, tight and breathless, from over yonder where he had vanished. I took quick, long steps, three of them, and looked down and saw what had gone with him.

He'd stood at the very edge of that shelf to pick the cedar, and a hunk of it must have broken off under his feet and sent him down into a fall, but not all the way down. It was shadowed below there, but I could see that he'd been able to grab hold. There were his two hands, bunched hard to hang onto two tufts of plants rooted into the rock. But past his hands hung the rest of him straight into the black shadows, hung above a long, long drop to the far below I couldn't make out. It was like a pit of blackness that he tried to keep out of, tried not to fall into, as he hung to those plants.

I was down on my knees right the next second, a-bending myself far down into that night-dark deepness to reach for him. But he was farther below me. I flung myself flat on my face and wallowed to where my head came over that crumbly ledge so I could look down. My nose was full of the greeny smell of the ferns all round and under me. I stretched my two arms down, as far as I could make them go.

My right fingertips touched the cuff of Reuben Manco's shirt. I hunched a tad on forward and put out my right hand one more inch and got hold of his tight-pulled wrist. I could feel the hard tendons of it, like wires. I gave thanks that I had good, big hands for such a grab, that they hadn't given out on me during that hard climb. I stretched my left arm down, too, until my left hand found and closed on his right wrist. I jammed my toes down among the ferns, as hard as I could, to keep hold on the slippy rock.

"Steady now, Chief," I said down to him, not loud, a-saving my breath for what must be done. "Let me couple hard onto you."

As I said that, I did it. I squeezed his wrists in my hands. I thought I could feel the blood in him as it beat in those cordy wrists I held, and I knew there was slick sweat betwixt them and the hard grip of my hands. I mustn't let them slip off away from me.

Flat I wallowed myself on that ledge, and I prayed it wouldn't crumble any farther. I pressed out my body to get as strong a hold on that ledge as I could. It was like as if I printed my shape into the rock under the ferns. No point in a-letting him go, no point in both of us to go over.

"Now, if you can," I wheezed over the rock into his face. "Let go that brush with your right hand and grab it to hold my wrist there. Grab with all you've got in you."

He didn't make a sound. He just did what I bid him. I felt his hard fingers as they closed on my arm like a noose of rope drawn tight.

"Now, if you've got a good grip there, do the same thing with your other hand," I told him. "Your left hand. Get my right wrist in it and hang on with both hands, hard."

He made that second switch, too. Now I could feel that I had his whole weight onto my stretched arms and hands. He hung, dead weight, down there, a right heavy thing to keep hold of, there in the bright night with me flat amongst the ferns and him on the dangle just below me.

What must I do next? One thing was certain sure, I couldn't spend any long length of time a-studying what it was. I had to work on just hunches. I didn't dare double up my arms to heave; that might could break his sweaty grip on me, or my grip on his, or both those things. I clung hard to my hold on him and worked a knee forward, a-being careful not to hunch myself up behind.

That knee found a knob of rock to shove against, and I was glad in my heart for that little help amongst all the slickness. I moved my other knee the same way, till I lay there with my legs drawn up tight under me like a cricket.

"Get set now, Chief," I whispered into the shadows where he hung above all the nothing. "I'm a-going to yank you up out of that. Be dead sure you clamp those two holds you've got. Jam your nails into me if you've got to, but don't let go. I'll take three breaths, and then—"

I took a breath, deep. Another breath. A third. In my heart I said some sort of prayer, though just what it was I couldn't remember later, a prayer to whoever or whatever might hear.

And I caught the third breath inside me. I jammed my knees down hard, I pulled all the strength I could into the muscles of my shoulders and back, and then I heaved myself up on my knees. I felt my chest come up from the brim of that devilish drop.

As I rose, I yanked Reuben Manco's wrists up with me. Still I didn't dare bend my arms. I surged away from the ledge where I knelt on it. I felt my back muscles crawl and hump, and next instant I slammed down, full sprawl, on one side. Just as I did that, Reuben Manco came a-flying up out of the dark and the emptiness and hit against me, then rolled clear. He was safe, safe.

And safe and limp we lay there all amongst the mashed ferns. We didn't move except to gulp in lungfuls of air, breathe it out, gulp in more. I knew that I was one big run of sweat from hair to foot. I felt a breeze on my face, a cool breeze. It felt right good there.

Reuben Manco was first to speak.

"*Aho*," he managed, betwixt breaths. "Thank you. Thank you, John. Thank you, my brother."

His hand groped over from where he lay. It took hold of my hand, as hard as it had held my wrist when he hung below the ledge.

And well I knew that when he called me his brother, he meant that thing. Meant it, though he was old enough to be my father, my father who'd died and been lost to me long ago, before I could truly know him.

IX

After a moment or two I had my breath back. I sat up and then Reuben Manco sat up too.

"Let's take a minute or so to get rid of the shakes," he said. "We can talk about the next step and what we may have to face. John, you saved my life. I won't forget it, not if I die tonight or if I live to be a hundred and ten."

"Go ahead and forget it right now, Chief," I said back. "You saved my own life down below yonder, when you killed that big old boar pig that was a-fixing to kill me."

"No." He shook his black hair in the moonlight. "You could have escaped. Standing where you did, you kept his attention so that I could strike him from the side. But when I fell down there I couldn't ever have come out if you hadn't pulled me out." He grinned at me. "My brother," he said.

I got up on my feet and looked at that sloping way with the trees on it. "What's a-waiting there?" I wondered out loud.

"That's what we must find out," said Reuben Manco, as he stood up beside me. "So far, we've made our way past two of the promised perils. There should be five more to get away from. They'll be set there for us."

He took a step or two. "Come on, John," he said.

So we headed along together, under the pouring glow of that moon up yonder.

Up the slope we went. Reuben Manco pointed out the

way we had to go through the trees. It wasn't a hard path in that kind of bright night, more so because Reuben Manco remembered so well where he was a-heading. On the far side, the way flattened out some. It was open there, with a big growth of plants, almost like a garden.

From what I could see of them, they were mullein stalks, grown up close together and the most of them I'd ever seen together in one place. They hiked themselves up in spikes as high as my knee or higher. Their leaves were soft-looking, hairy. To me it was like as if they come close round my legs as I walked. They sort of rubbed there, like cats that wanted to be petted. It was like as if they whispered to me. I looked down at them. They seemed all of a sudden to go dark and gloomy. That was because of a rag of cloud that went a-sailing across the sky, then flew off again to let the light come strongish down.

All I'd ever heard for a certain fact about the mullein was an old story, how if you stomped down a stalk of it to point to the home of the one you loved, it would grow up strong again if she was true to you. I'd never felt called on to try that trick, because I'd never wondered myself about Evadare. Other than that tale, I'd never heard tell if a mullein was good or bad for aught in this world, except it was hard to kill out when it tried to take your garden.

We waded through those things and got out the other side. We stopped again for a moment.

"That sure enough wasn't one of the perils," I guessed.

"Hardly," said Reuben Manco, "though I don't remember that sort of growth here when I was a boy. I did have a feeling that those weeds were trying to talk to us, maybe to tell us to go back."

"Seemed to me they sort of whispered, but I couldn't

make out air a mumbling word of it," I said. "Might could the Druid folks have had aught to do with mullein stalks?"

"Not that ever I heard," Reuben Manco replied me. "Though the mullein was originally an old-world plant. It got imported to America and made itself right at home everywhere. But there's nothing about the mullein in any work I ever saw about the Druids, and I've seen many. With submission, I think I know about the Druids."

He sure enough did, I allowed to myself, and likewise he knew about a sight of other things, too. He was good to have along on a chancy job. "Where's our trail now?" I inquired him.

"Right on ahead."

He moved out on it, though it was nothing easy to make out in that sort of light. I followed him along through the rest of the empty stretch, and in amongst some low bushes that had bunches of thorns. One thorn raked across the back of my hand, and I felt a spot of blood come out there, but I nair said aught about it. We worried through the bushes, and some open-growing trees beyond, no great matter to pass amongst them. Then we came to another halt, to look at what we saw just ahead.

We'd come out in another clearing, with woods grown up to the right and left of us, and the moon a-coming down from where it had climbed. But right there in our way, maybe fifty-sixty yards on, was a whiteness that stirred and rippled.

At first sight, I reckoned it was a wall of some kind, a-stretching out away into the trees this side and that. But then I saw the movement in the night. It had a stir to it, the way you see on still water when a little breeze touches it. The soft white stuff didn't look much higher than a man's head to me, and not rightly solid, either.

"What in the name of gracious is that?" I inquired myself and Reuben Manco both.

He never replied me aught. Instead he went forward, slow and careful as a hunter when he's out a-stalking a deer. When he got a few steps closer in, he stopped and had another look, this way and then that.

"It seems to be something like smoke," he said then, "or a thick fog. Right there, in that single belt of space."

I, too, took a good look at the stuff. If it was smoke or fog, it hung in almighty close to itself. It gave off a little reflection, not much. It didn't seem to be slick enough for that. It stirred, and it waited.

"Why don't we move off to the left here?" I said. "Maybe we can find our way round it."

"That would never work," Reuben Manco allowed. "Look, it stretches deep into the thick woods there. Even if we found a way around, perhaps we'd get lost from the way we must follow."

"The way we must follow," I said the words after him.

"I'd theorize that this is more Druidism," Reuben Manco went on. "They claimed that they could control weather—rain, wind, snow, all things like that. In England, thick mist is familiar. Sometimes it's forbidding. And if it's there to forbid us, we're here to face it."

He turned his face to me, and I saw the lights and shadows on it.

"Are you game?" he asked me.

"Sure, I'm game, if you are," I said back, for that was all I could say unless that I'd quit and let the Voths do what they might choose to do with Holly and Luke. "You know, Chief, I've seen my share of fog on these mountains, daytime and nighttime both, but I've nair seen the like of that in all my born days."

"I repeat, it's apt to be a Druidic specialty, more or less."

"And you tell me that we've got to try to shove through it," I said.

"John," he said, a deep rumble, the way Indians do when they're pure down serious, "I've heard it said that the powers of darkness can't prevail against a pure heart. My heart may not be pure, but I hope it's brave."

"Same here," I said.

"All right, here goes. Let's try to stick close together in there."

We walked toward that white quilty wall of mist, side by side. It looked like piled-up suds before us, all the suds in this world. The air turned sort of steamy as we came close, and it had a warm, rotty smell, the sort you get from an old straw stack that's been rained on for a month or so. The closer we walked, the dimmer the light blurred to my eyes. We came right up against it, and into it we walked.

"Stay close," I could hear Reuben Manco beside me. His voice sounded like as if it came through a muffler over his mouth. I took another step in, another. I felt a sort of slippy mushiness under the soles of my shoes.

By then I couldn't rightly see a thing. It wasn't a blackness to my eyes, the way it would have been in a dark room, but I just couldn't see. My ears took on a funny, blocked feeling, the way your ears get when you swim to the bottom of a pond. I tried to say something to Reuben Manco, but my voice didn't want to come out and be heard. I moved along, step by step, my feet a-feeling the way. The ground, or whatever might have been there instead of ground, had gone mushy-soft, sorry to my feet. I almost slipped and fell, and then I almost slipped and fell again.

I hadn't better go down, I told myself flat out, because there might not be a getting up. I tried and tried to feel the way along with my big, thick shoes. My legs moved slowly. It was tough work to move them, like when you wade in deep water with mud at the bottom of it. My head felt all stopped up, like as if some doctor had jammed it full of cotton. I felt dizzy, there was a gone-away feeling in my mind. And there was more than that to trouble me. Things in that mist, under and all through that mist, seemed to wiggle themselves in around me, seemed to want to grab hold of me.

It wasn't like as if they had hands or like that. They kept on to try to wrap themselves on me, sort of, round my legs and elbows and waist, like snakes. I yanked myself free of them, while I fought to keep my feet with all the slipperiness and the dizziness. I wondered myself in my heart, should I ought to say a prayer. Instead of that, while I squashed on ahead by steps and kept on a-dragging myself free of all those snaky clutches and touches, I found that I thought of Evadare. I thought of what a little bitty thing she was, but how brave and how true-loving, and of how maybe she was a-thinking of me her own self, wherever she was, right then and there. Maybe that helped.

But gentlemen, it was almighty hard, almighty bad. I sort of half-strangled in the thick, blinding damp. I could scarcely draw me a breath in it. My stopped-up head wanted to droop on my neck. I knew if I let it do that, I'd sway to one side or the other, and down I'd go. And if I went down, likely I'd stay down. I had the notion I could hear voices. They said something like *huhh, huhh,* though that might could have been the blood a-beating in my crammed ears. Once a sort of wiggly arm-thing touched my face and slid down to my neck. I reckon it tried to wrap itself round and take hold there. *Huhh, huhh,* beat the voices. But before I could put up my own hand to fight that arm off, it was gone away. I was pure down grateful it went.

I don't reckon it was a right long time, nor yet any great distance, for me to slap and stumble forward through that hellacious mess. But it seemed like miles and hours till all of a sudden the fog thinned a little bit, then thinned another bit, and then I could see. And then I could breathe. And then I could take steps out on what was firmer footing, and then I was somehow free of it, and glad and happy to see the ground and the trees and the moon-glowing sky.

I dragged a big gulp of air into my lungs and stomped with my feet. I shook my head and it came clear a little. I remembered Reuben Manco.

"Chief!" I yelled out my loudest.

No answer from him.

I gulped more air and swung myself round to look at that mist from the side I'd come out on. It hung there, clotted together, hung like a curtain, a sudsy fence. No sign of Reuben Manco in it, either.

"Chief!" I hollered again.

That time I reckoned I did hear something, like the bubbly noise made by a drowning man, and deep at one point in the mist I saw a stir. It churned there. Maybe somebody tried to struggle in it.

I took one second to tell myself I'd been in there and come clear once, so I should ought to be able to make it again. No more than a second, though. I headed right back in, like a frog a-sliding into a pool. I stabbed down my feet to keep the bottom under me and I groped out to right and left with my hands.

I came on Reuben Manco almost at once. I got a good clamp on his arm and his shoulder. Out I went backward, the way I'd headed in. There was a weaving push all round the both of us, wiggly arms or the like. I shoved with my back at those things, the way you try to slam your way through a thicket of pole-sized trees. They gave off from my shove. Light glimmered again and I was free, my knees a-bucking with the effort. I dragged Reuben along with me, into the moonlight.

He could barely stand on his feet. He looked soaked all over, the way he'd be if he'd stood under a shower bath with all his clothes on. And, when I took time at last to notice, I was soaked all over too. Our shirts and pants hung wet and draggy to our bodies.

He mopped his face and blinked in the pale light we'd won through to. "It's getting to be routine with you, saving me," he managed to say.

"I'd made it out this side, and heard you in there and went back for you," I said.

He stood and breathed in air to clear his lungs. His hands rubbed his neck.

"There was a death grip on me," he told me. "It was choking me. I couldn't breathe."

I looked him up and down. He was a-getting hold of himself again. "Whatever it was in yonder kept on a-trying to put its hold on me," I said, "but it didn't try to choke me. Just once, there was something here at my neck." I put a hand there. "It just touched me and then it yanked away, like as if it had been burned."

He stepped close to me and put up his own hand to my throat. "Yes," he said, "and it was because of that. Holly's charm you've been wearing, the wise, strong power of the mammoth image. It must have protected you, John, stood your friend."

"Well, maybe so," I said, because I could see what he meant. "Anyway, the two of us got through all right, and that means we've whipped the third bad thing put in our way."

He turned round to look at that wall of foamy mist. It didn't seem to be so thick right then.

"I would call it a very special, very intricate obstacle, quite originally conceived and achieved," he allowed, in that way he had that put me in mind of a teacher with a science class. "The mist, many times concentrated, and within it what must have been certain malevolent spirits of the mist. But suppose I stop being the learned lecturer. If that was the third peril, we must consider what the fourth may be."

We'd come out in what was pretty much open country again, a fairly level piece of it for a mountaintop. Ahead of us lay stretches of rocks, mostly flat and deep-set in the earth, near about like a pavement. We started along them. Reuben Manco squinted up at the sky.

"By the position of the moon and stars, I estimate that we have a good two hours until midnight," he said. "That should give us time enough before they start whatever they propose to do with their prisoners. Even if we find ourselves doing some sort of swim again."

But I wasn't a-looking up at the sky. I looked to where I thought I saw some sort of light ahead. It wasn't moonlight, either. It had a sort of reddish shine to it.

"Looks to be like fire up yonder, Chief," I guessed. Do you reckon they're a-lighting up a patch of woods to show us the way?"

He, too, gave it the eye.

"Fire," he repeated me. "Yes. That's exactly the color of that radiance." He hummed in his throat as he walked. "Suppose you let me adopt the flavory vernacular of those mountain songs you do so well, John. We've made our way out of a mist that was more or less like the bottom of the worst lake they could pour for us with their sorceries. But now, just a short jaunt along the way—it's like a mountain spiritual I've heard played and sung."

He sang it himself, and his voice was tuneful:

God gave Noah the rainbow sign,
No more water, the fire next time—

"I know that one, Chief," I said to him. "I've played it myself and I've always liked it. But it doesn't sound like a threat to me. The names of God and Noah sound more like some kind of good promise."

"Let's devoutly hope so."

All that while, we'd been a-walking. The red glow got stronger among the rocks up there where we were headed. That wouldn't be the fire next time.

It would be the fire this time.

X

"I'm obliged to admire those Voth brothers for several qualities," Reuben Manco told me, calm as ever. "They have special powers, and they know how to use them. They have enterprise, they have a sort of dedicated spirit that we'd better match in ourselves. However, they aren't being truly original, not just now."

"I don't follow you," I said.

"Look there, John." He pointed. "They've changed the substance of their wall, but not the shape of it. Nor, in the important sense, the position of it. We're barred by another wall, fire instead of mist."

We were a-walking closer to it, all the time. It was fire, that was the truth. Big red tongues of it licked up, right out of the rocky height of the mountain. Once I'd seen pictures of an eclipse of the sun, how the moon darkens out the whole red ball of it, and how the sun's flames jump out of the dark where the moon doesn't get itself in the way. It looked a right much like that I, thought. Only it was a straight line of flames, not a circle of them.

Reuben Manco had told the truth. The way it had been with the mist was the same way with the fire. It reached itself away to left and right, that wall, clean across the bald where we were a-making our way to it, and each end lost itself among bunches of trees farther off there. It didn't seem to blaze the trees up, it just danced in them. What was it that Reuben Manco had come up with?

There'd be no thought about making a turn to go far off and maybe get round it. Because it was set up in our path. We had to follow that path on through it, or either on over it. That was a rule of some sort or other. I'd been up against magic in my time, and the thought made sense to me.

"It may be just as well that we got all soaked through by the fog they put in our way back there," said Reuben Manco.

I took a look behind us as we walked. The mist didn't seem to hang so high and solid and white. I thought it looked to be faded down. Maybe it just wasn't supposed to be there, except to try to stop us.

"What'll we try to do about that fire?" I inquired him. "It jumps up higher and hotter air step we take to it. Are we supposed just to walk through?"

"No," he replied me, "we're supposed to be kept back. But the fog was to keep us back, and we walked through that."

While we talked, we came along past a clump of big old mountain ash trees, and beyond those we had a good notion of what sort of thing we had to do if we were to get across.

That wall of red fire had a kind of foundation, I'm honest to tell you. The mountain was ripped open there, a big, deep gully in it from side to side all that way right and left, with jagged rocks along the edge to us. Up poured those flames, a-squirting up there, a-hopping and a-flashing. I could make out little bits of blue and green in the red of them. They must have been eighteen-twenty feet high, right there ahead of us. Maybe they got high because we'd come so near to them, maybe they could tell we were there. We came close enough to feel the heat of them on our wet skins.

"What do we do, Chief?" I asked him again.

"We cross," he replied me. "We can do it. They promised us seven perils, and this is only the fourth. If they put seven in the way, they must have thought we might get past some of them—as many as six of them. The seventh will be something special."

"I could wish to know how to get past this one," I had to say. Because, to me, it looked like one of the seven entrances to hell you hear tell about in the old folks's tales. That big wild boar pig Reuben Manco had stuck down below could have roasted to a turn in that fire, while a man was a-singing three verses of a song.

Reuben Manco moved forward again, careful with his feet, his face sharpened against the hotness, and I went with him. We got to where we could make out things clear and plain.

That ditch the fire jumped up from was a deep one. The rocks down inside it seemed to glower and wink, like red-hot iron in a blacksmith forge. And I reckoned the ditch was eight feet across at least. There'd be no way just to walk through it, even if the wet in our clothes would help us. One step from the edge would take a man down, I didn't like to study how far or where to.

"What do we do?" I inquired him one more time.

"Do?" he said me my word back. "There's only one thing to do, jump across. I feel that I could do it. Try it, anyway."

He made another step, but I grabbed him by the wrist.

"Hold on," I said. "Let's take all the difference we can. Let's do something to help that jump."

"What are you talking about, John?"

"Come back here to these ash trees. And let me have the lend of that tomahawk you fetched along."

I saw his eyes crinkle up, a-wondering himself what I

115

meant, but he pulled the tomahawk out of its place in his belt and handed it across to me.

I headed for the ash clump. I looked at one after another of the trees, feeling them with my free hand. I chose out a sapling, good and tall and say four inches through just above the roots. I looked it up and down. Then I planted my feet and swung the tomahawk and made a deep cut into the wood.

"Why this timber-cutting, John?" Reuben Manco wanted me to tell him.

"I want a long, straight piece of this tree," I said, and swung the tomahawk again to knock out a chip. "There's a kind of jump you do with a pole." Another chip. It flew off, white as china in the moonlight. "I've seen young fellows do it at school, what they call a track meet."

"Pole-vaulting?" he yipped out. "That's brilliant, John, it's the right thing. I'm ashamed that you had to remind me."

"You've likely seen it done," I said, chopping.

"Why, man, I've done it myself. I was a pole-vaulter, long ago at Dartmouth." He thought that over. "It was only an intramural meet, though. Not varsity."

The live ash wood was no soft thing to chop through with just that light tomahawk, but I worked my way round and round above the roots, like a beaver. I had wood chewed out on all sides. Reuben Manco came and leaned his weight to it. More hacking, and it began to creak and crack when he shoved. Finally it broke clean off. I bent over and swung the tomahawk to set it free from the stump.

Then Reuben Manco took the tomahawk and went to work on the branches. They were tough, too, but clearing them away was quicker to get done. We lopped off the top of the sapling, where it was maybe near about the thickness of my wrist from one side to the other. It was a nice straight pole, a good sixteen feet long as I judged. But when I picked it up, it felt to be as heavy as iron.

"I'll go first," said Reuben Manco. "I've done pole-vaulting. I understand it."

"Nothing doing, Chief, I was the one thought of the thing. I get first jump."

He spread his hands and hunched his shoulders, giving in but not wanting to. He took the pole and hefted it.

"Better go with the big end first, you can get a better grip on it where it's thinner," he said. "Let it carry you as high as you can make it, and that should put you on the far side. John, you're my brother now. Do it and get there safely."

"Thanks," I said. "I do my best most times."

I put up a hand to shield my face from the heat and walked in as close as I could get without a-scorching myself. The flames jumped up there, high as a barn roof. At the edge of the ditch I saw some solid rocks all bunched together, and that's where I told myself to plant my pole to go up. Back I came, and pointed out the place to Reuben Manco.

"Good," he said, like a coach. "Now make it a steady run, long steps, and be ready to fly up when the end of the pole goes home at those rocks. Every god there is in heaven is watching you, John, giving you strength."

"Thanks," I said again, and picked up that pole.

I stood a moment with it hiked up in my two hands while I studied the way I must run in. The ground looked more or less smooth and firm, all the way there. I gulped in some air and ran forward.

The heat slapped my face like a shovelful of hot sand. I knew I mustn't slack off. In I ran, saw where to slam down the point, and down I slammed it and jumped my best.

I flew up and up, the pole a-carrying me. As I rose into

the air, that good ash sapling sprang me higher. I seemed like a flag that fluttered in a wind. I saw red light all round me, felt the curling flames hit at me, a scorching tug at me all over. I hoped with all my heart that my jump was long enough, that I wouldn't pop down into that burning ditch. And all of a sudden I was down on solid ground beyond, just one stumble then a-running from the heat of the flames, while with me I dragged that pole of ash. Steam jumped up from my wet clothes into my face.

"John!" yelled Reuben Manco's voice. "Are you all right? Did you make it?"

The flames roared a noise like wind. I put up my own voice loud enough to yell back.

"I'll fling this pole back for you, Chief," I told him. "I'm a-tying something to it that maybe helped me through—look for it when it comes!"

From off my neck I hiked the elephant charm. The leather thong was still clammy wet, though it had just come through fire. I tied it tight round the pole, about three feet from the small end.

"Stand by yonder to get it!" I hollered him.

I upped that heavy chunk of wood and balanced it on my left palm. Then I walked in as close as that jumping, blazing heat would let me. With all the strength I could get up, I flung the pole like a spear. It sailed through those flames like a big, long bird.

"I've got it!" I heard Reuben Manco call out through the fire. "Here I come!"

I pulled back to wait, all I could do.

I couldn't make him out through the red curtain of fire. It jumped up like as if a high wind blew into it. I heard it crackle, a hungry, ugly crackling. Maybe my jump through there had done that to it. Maybe it was a-getting itself ready to gobble Reuben Manco.

"Here I come, John!" he yelled again, louder than the crackle.

I stood as close to that glaring, blinding heat as I could hold myself. It hurt my eyes to look into it, but I looked. Yonder came something, a dark something a-flying up high into the brightness. It hung there for what seemed a long second, while the tongues of flame licked all over it. Then it shoved on through the brightness to the side where I waited, and it came a-slamming down. It passed with its feet on the rocks and then it stumbled toward me and went down on one knee and one hand. As I ran close, Reuben Manco stood up.

I grabbed onto him to see was he all right. His clothes steamed, like mine. He shook me off and stooped down.

"Get that pole that helped us vault across," he wheezed at me. "It's picked up power from what it did."

I grabbed up the pole. It was scorched all over from its three trips through those flames. We moved back away from the heat and the glimmer.

"Does it occur to you, John, that the foggy, foggy dew is somewhat dried off our clothes?" said Reuben Manco.

I looked down at myself, while I carried the pole. Sure enough, what he'd said was true.

"The Voths didn't count on their foam barricade helping us against their fire barricade," Reuben Manco half-laughed. "In that particular, at least, they canceled one peril out with another. I ask myself if Cherokee magic wisdom, seasoned here in its own native land, may not be better than Druidic magic wisdom, transplanted here."

We stood off and looked back at the fire. It seemed to be a-burning lower. Or possibly it had looked higher and burninger when we'd been over yonder, at the other side of it.

"What about this pole you told me to fetch?" I asked. "It's a right heavy chunk of wood to wag along with us."

"You're right, and I did remark that it was much heavier than a true vaulting pole," said Reuben Manco. "But it served us against evil magic, and that gives it strength. Put it down here, John."

I did so. He squatted beside it and put his hand on it. He began to sing. I could hear him, but couldn't make out the words. They were Indian words, Cherokee words, a prayer of some kind as I figured. So I stood beside him and said a prayer of my own. In it, I reminded whoever might have an ear to the other end of the line that we two were up on Wolter Mountain, a-periling our lives every step, to help two other folks, young folks who didn't belong to be in their bad trouble.

After a minute or so that-a-way, Reuben Manco got up and pulled his tomahawk out of his belt.

"Ash wood," he said. "And it's stood our friend already, it's lifted us over their wall of fire. That makes it an ally. Ash was a sacred wood to the Druidic priests in sacred times. Ash and oak and thorn—that was a pagan oath. It's in a song they call *Glasgerion*."

"I recollect I've heard that song, though I don't sing it myself," I told him. "I've always had it in mind that oak and ash and thorn meant the trees the cross was made out of, with the thorn for the crown of thorns."

"No, those were all trees of power before ever the Crucifixion took place. You've already heard considerable talk about the oak as a special object of veneration with the Druids. But maybe this ash will stand by us."

He set himself a-straddle of the pole and came down with the tomahawk, skillful as air woodcutter I'd ever seen. He made a split in the narrow end, chopped again and again, and then I took one split of it and he took the other. We put our man on it as hard as we could, and dragged that pole in two for several feet. Then Reuben

Manco cut off two chunks from the end he'd split, each about three feet long or so. He gave me one of them.

"It feels like a good club," I allowed, giving it a heft.

"We'll carry them along," he said, "no telling for what need."

Then he fumbled his canteen out of its carrying pouch. "Here, John," he said, and reached it to me. "We deserve a mouthful of water just now. I could wish it was a mouthful of that prime blockade down in the Forshay cabin."

"I could wish the same," I said, and drank. He took the canteen back and had a cut out of it in his turn. Both of us swished the water round and round in our mouths and let it seep down. That made us feel better.

"And here," said Reuben Manco. He took the elephant charm off of where it hung on his neck and passed it to me. "That's a help, too. Wear it and trust in it."

I slung the thong over my head and tucked the thing into my shirt.

"I make it four perils that we've met and somehow circumvented," said Reuben Manco as he pouched his canteen again. "Though perhaps circumventing isn't the exact term when sometimes you go straight through. We killed that wild boar sent to put his tusks into us. We escaped falling down that high cliff, or anyway I did when you pulled me up from where I hung. We half-waded, half-swam, through the mist. And we vaulted over the fire."

I took a look back at that fire. It seemed to be fading down into its gully.

"You reckon all these things are Druid doings," I said.

"Manifestly they're Druidism," he nodded his black head. "The boar, I told you, was an animal of magic to the Celtic peoples. Steep heights of land were places of special power. The Druids knew and governed the spirits of mist and fog. And fire—it was sacred and mystical to the Druids and to almost everyone else. Even to the Cherokees, my people."

"If there was just one Voth to tackle—" I began.

"But there are two," he said. "Brothers. A pair of brothers, as wise partners in magic, can have more method and power than just two magicians working separately. I daresay there's a mathematical explanation if we had time to work it out. Two brothers, adept and prepared and determined, can present more than a simple double problem."

"We're even and square with them, anyway," I said. "You called me your brother, Chief, and I reckon if you say that, it's so. And it might could be that our kind of brothers—the kind that chooses out one another—have a chance to turn out better than just brothers born to the same father and mother, brothers that have to do the best they can with just their own blood kin."

Reuben Manco laughed at that one. He sure enough laughed, in the moony night on that mountain stuck so full of perils brought out and set against us. I saw his white teeth shine. He put out his hand and gave me a good whack on the shoulder.

"John, you're magnificent," he said.

"Oh," I said, "I'm not about to claim magnificence to me. Mostly, all my life, I've just strove to be a natural man."

He laughed again, and gave me another whack.

"Whatever you are, you aren't an unnatural man," he vowed. "We've put ourselves into a desperate situation together, but since we're in it, I'll say to the world that I couldn't ask for a better partner."

Then he looked ahead of us. The fire behind us made it

seem darker off yonder. I made out belts of trees, and here and there rocks a-sticking up amongst them.

"Come on, John," he said, "let's see what comes next."

As we started out, side by side again, I began to wonder myself about what the fifth peril would be. Then I told myself inside me, better not go to guess at that. Because, guessing at one thing, you might could start a-fixing to meet just that one thing. And all the while another thing, a worse thing, might really be on the wait for you.

XI

It was high time to look ahead, all right. There was more light than before, with the moon swum farther up the sky. We could see that the balded-out place on Wolter Mountain top ran on into where trees grew up a rise yonder. Those trees looked right thick-grown, a-hanging darker and closer to one another than the ones we'd come through so far.

When I started in to take longer steps so as to go faster, Reuben Manco hung back. So I slowed down to stay with him.

"There's no headlong hurry for us, John," he said. "We mustn't get there tired."

That made me to take note that we'd been through some right tiring things. The scramble along through the woods from the Forshay place, then that squirrel climb up the cliff, the heave and strain to get Reuben Manco up from where he'd fallen down, then the soggy mist and what had amounted to a swim in the deepest part of a pond. The jump over the fire hadn't taken so much to do, but the other things had sure enough told on us.

"You're right, as usual," I allowed to him. "But I feel right spry on my feet just now."

"As I've said, we have plenty of time before midnight," he repeated to me. "At this point, I doubt if we have to travel more than two miles or so. We'll either be where we're going in ample time to stop what we must stop, or we'll never get there at all. The perils still waiting ahead may account for us if we don't be careful."

As I walked slower with him, I saw the thing he meant. It was a-getting better all the time to be out there in the night with Chief Reuben Manco and hear what he had to say about our job, about air other thing he cared to mention to me. I took me a look back. That string of fire that had jumped up so high and hot looked sort of dimmed down now, low and fainty and near about to die into itself.

"Yes, you can see that those flames are dwindling," said Reuben Manco. "They were bright and fierce when we had to jump through them, but we did that. Now they're no good any more, they're useless to our enemies. The same with the belt of fog; we had no more than made our way through that than it began to dissolve behind us."

Which was flat the truth, I reckoned.

"That fire and that mist, they weren't natural," I spoke my own thought. "Not like that old boar pig, down yonder at the foot of the mountain. He was as natural as air living soul could call for."

"He wasn't quite natural in that he wasn't truly American," said Reuben Manco. "He was an example of a stock recently imported, which causes trouble. I read in a newspaper the other day about an effort to ship those wild boars out of the parks to where hunters can kill them. I can give you what the park superintendent said, almost word for word. He pointed out that, because that species of wild boar is non-native, it disrupts our natural environment."

I thought that over, a long enough time to take two steps and a breath.

"You might could say the same about white men a-coming here to America," I offered him then. "The Indians had lived here all those thousands of years, and nair ruined things. It's taken the white folks to do that, all across America."

He laughed one of his laughs that you scarce could catch. "I hear you say that with admiration, John. It supports my notion that you have Indian blood in your veins. Anyway, you think for yourself. And if a man can't do that, he isn't really thinking."

"There may be a whole lot in what you say," I agreed him.

He pointed on ahead of us with his stick. "You can see quite a belt of forest along there. It's heavily grown up here on the height, more than I remember. No timber-cutter has ever come near it, by its looks. What can we expect from that particular growth?"

"I don't rightly know how to answer that," I said. "Maybe oak and ash and thorn."

He shot me a quick, scowly look. "Whatever made you say those names?"

"Likely because you mentioned them, just a while back."

"Yes, so I did." He hiked the chunk of ash tree in his brown hand. "Those are three powerful trees, John. At least, so Druidic religious philosophy sees them. We were speaking of non-native influences abroad here tonight. Druidism is one of those, and you and I hadn't better stop with defeating it just locally. We'd better close it out. Completely."

And he bit his teeth together on that. You could hear them click. I looked up again at the moon. The light was strong, but it made things look worse, look scarier, than the sunlight would. Special bad just then was the look of those dark trees we were headed for.

The way I do now and then, I thought of something to make into a song. I whispered words to myself:

> Moon over Wolter Mountain,
> What makes your face so white?
> Strange things past all our countin'
> Sneak out here in the night—

Reuben Manco spoke. He'd been a-looking up at the moon, too.

"She used to be a goddess," he said. "Not just the Druids called her that, not just Europeans and Asiatics. The Cherokees did. Sometimes I feel a touch of sadness when I think that men have gone to the moon and proved her to be just a silent, dusty rock."

"Do the Voths think the moon's a goddess?" I wondered him.

"Undoubtedly they do. That's why you and I are out here tonight, to prevent them from worshiping the moon in their balefully interesting way."

We kept on our walk toward where those trees grew. I thought of more words of the song, even something of a tune to put them to:

> We travel our way and wonder
> If all of our hopes will fail;
> Moon in the sky up yonder,
> What makes your face so pale?

If so happen I'd fetched along my guitar, I could have tried it out, smoothed up the words and the tune, made a sure enough song of it. Only, if I'd fetched my guitar, up that steep rough climb and on through the mist and through the fire, it likely wouldn't have been such a great shakes of a guitar by now.

Even in the light of the moon we'd spoken of, those

trees looked black as ink. I reckoned to myself that I'd nair seen trees that dark-leafed, that secret to themselves. I'd always liked trees of all kinds, I'd felt I belonged along with them. Maybe it was a bad feeling now because people, the wrong ones, had fooled with trees on that mountain, made them to do wrong. I walked with Reuben Manco toward them.

We got close enough to make out how near one another the trees looked. They grew close up, side by side, like the poles of a fence. Their branches all twined and twisted together. And the moon nair put a beam to them. Reuben Manco took me by the arm to make me stand.

"Let me go there first," he said, and I let him. He walked up under the branches of those close-growing trees. He walked slow, he was springy on his toes, like a man set ready to pull back quick if he had to.

"One thing is certain," he said over his shoulder to me. "Nothing like this grove was here when I used to come up as a boy." He stood almost against the big stem of a tree. "This is an oak," he named it.

"Oak," I repeated him, a-coming a few steps closer, with in my mind what he'd told me about oaks and Druids.

"And, twisting around it," he said next, "some branches of thorn."

"Oak and ash and—" I started to say.

"Just stop right there," he spoke, quick and sharp, to cut me off. "Be careful with those particular words in this situation." He turned his back on that fence of dark tree trunks. "Well, John," he said, "there's nothing for us to do but go through here."

Right like that he said it, in the calm way he'd said things all along. I nodded to him in the moonlight. I'd already heard how he felt there must be no a-going round,

128

no dodging a peril that-a-way. *Perils,* I repeated the word inside myself. I was a-starting to get a little small bit tired of perils. They wore you out, they wet you down and they scorched you. It got common, I felt as I wondered myself just how long a good man's luck could hold out against perils. Hardly forever, anyway.

Reuben Manco had gone back up against those trees. He poked with his ash stick into a space betwixt two of them. It didn't look bigger than a hand's width. "Here," he said to me, and next moment he'd squeezed himself in.

With him shoved out of sight that-a-way, I naturally had to follow. I fought hard to get through that little small slice of an opening in bewixt two tall, rough trunks. Oak they were, by the feel of them. The darkness seemed to jump in round us like a blanket flung close.

Mostly I do all right in the dark. Like maybe I've mentioned one time or other, there's an old notion that a child born in the night can feel his way anywhere, and my birth time had been near about the stroke of midnight back yonder. Maybe that's what put my feet to a good feel of their way amongst the roots twined under them. But, gentlemen, it was no easy trick to work among the trunks.

I put out my ash stick to seek for openings where I might get through. I scraped my shoulder and my cheek on branch stobs. I felt with my other hand. I ask myself today, did those tree trunks have a strange feel to my finger, did some of them seem to have skin on them instead of natural bark? Did one or other of them have a throbby beat in them, like blood in a living thing? It might could have been I was imagining stuff the like of that, a-being up there on creepy Wolter Mountain that-a-way, and closed in now by tree with branches crisscrossed to hold me, thorns to rake and jab at me. That sort of thing, after what I'd already been through with those other perils, on my way to do what we'd decided must be done. But if it was my imagination, then it was right powerful for strength.

I feared I'd lost touch of Reuben Manco, but then I came almost up against his back, my hand on it though I couldn't rightly make him out. Branches crowded between us. Maybe he'd stopped so I could catch up, maybe he'd been caught there. I didn't get round to asking him later on.

"Use your ash stick, John," he said, in a breathy whisper. "Perhaps it can help you some way. Push in now, there where it seems thickest."

It seemed thickest all the way round us right then. Over us the branches strung and wove themselves together, dark and heavy, a-making a thatch like a roof. I couldn't see one scrap of the light that moon made in the sky somewhere else, the light we'd had to help us so far. All we had was a blackness so thick it seemed to close on us like muddy water, and trees and sprouts and branches close round us like as if they were woven tight as a basket.

I pushed with my stick, the way he'd told me. And I could swear, it made a way for me. Reuben Manco moved a step ahead. Likely he was up to the same trick. A branch of thorns came down on my neck and shoulder. It didn't fall, it came down; and it raked me deep, like the claws of an animal, I thought. When I tried to yank clear of it, those thorns shoved themselves tighter, deeper. I hit at it with the stick, and right off it let me go.

"Ash is on our side, John," Reuben Manco got tight words out to me. He was a-striving with all his might, too. "Ash—it will work for one man as well as another."

Because he'd prayed over it, because ash had helped us jump and sail up over that wall of fire, he knew that thing. I harked to him, and felt better. I made a swing with my stick at a great big tree. I swear on my soul it pulled off away from me and let me step past it. I vow, that was a creepy thing, a tree on the move, even on the move out of my way.

All that time, thorns raked into us here and there and up and down. My shirt was ripped, my pants were ripped. Thorns stabbed amongst my hair, they clutched there like fingers. They pushed into my scalp, they seemed to grope for my eyes. I whirled my stick round my head to drive them away. Without that stick and Reuben Manco's prayer on it, what might could have happened? I don't care to wonder that.

Perhaps our ash sticks made the ash trees in there more or less leave us be, but the oaks and thorns wanted to hold onto us there, do something to us. A-batting and a-whacking, I wished my eyes could get used to that dark. I felt branches all round my knees and ankles, like as if they tried to catch me in their forks or wrap round me. They were like snakes. They had life, and I pure down hated them. I wished with all my heart I had an axe, or even Reuben Manco's tomahawk. Though that might could have been the wrong thing.

Anyway, the ash club likely was better than an axe. Reuben Manco must have reckoned that, for he never drew out the tomahawk. We fought on, deeper and deeper among the trees, with the big wonder in our hearts if ever they'd come to an end at all. Sometimes it was like a-being in the middle of where a house had fallen in on you, boards and beams and timbers and rafters all round and over you. They shoved, they dug. I had to hike the muscle of my arm to use my stick to prod me some room in all that shoving, smashing clutter.

I reckon I must have been bleeding from a dozen places when I saw a little scrap of soft brightness somewhere ahead. I shoved toward it, among those crowding, grabbing trees. Branches tried to hang onto me, but I fought loose of them. I came out into open ground betwixt two big, rough oak trunks, and for a second there I thought I'd fall down. I leaned hard on my ash stick and gulped in air, the way I'd done when I got out of the mist.

"Are you all right, John?" the voice of Reuben Manco inquired me.

I looked round and saw him then, half a dozen steps into the open. The moon gave me a good clear sight of him. His black hair was flung air which-a-way, and one of his sleeves was ripped from the shoulder to the cuff. His elbow poked through. He was a-resting on his stick, the way I did.

"So we've made it past another peril," he said, as quiet and cool as if he'd been a-mentioning the time of day.

"I reckon so," I replied him, "and we look as if we'd fought our way out of a hard times party."

I dabbed at my own hair. A thorn was still caught in it, as big as a six-penny nail and as sharp as a wasp's stinger. I looked down at where blood showed, black wet, on my sleeves in the moonlight. My shirt was torn half off me, my pant legs were torn. I felt my cheek. It was chopped open and bleeding.

"Look back at those trees," Reuben Manco bade me.

I turned round, my legs steady now. By heaven, the trees looked just like a grove of trees. They weren't set as thick and tight as I well knew they'd been.

"We won past them, and the power is departing from them," said Reuben Manco. "They were our fifth peril, John. Two more wait for us ahead. And quite likely they'll be the most perilous of all."

"You've got to give it to those Voth brothers," I made

out to remark. "They're a hard-working pair of somebodies, and that's the true word for us."

Reuben Manco laughed. It was a hard, ugly laugh this time.

"And I imagine their hard work and planning wasn't for nothing, John. Quite likely this fifth peril set things up for the sixth peril that will be coming."

"What way could it do that?" I asked.

"Look at how those thorns scratched and dug into our flesh," he said. "Look at the wounds all over us. Both of us are bleeding."

I studied my arms and hands and I felt my face. "I don't reckon I'm a-shedding enough blood to make me weak or the like of that." I swung that ash club he'd given me. "I can still use this."

"Will that ash club be enough?" he wondered us. "Look on ahead, John, the way we must go."

There was light enough to see right well. We stood and faced rocks now. Whatever trees we'd had to push through were all behind us. I saw roughish country, with chunks of dark stone shoved up in it, here and there. Those chunks looked like sheds and walls and houses, some way, put up by who could say what crazy-headed builders.

"Shoo, Chief, we can make it through there all right," I said at once. "I don't see air great steeps or heights. We may have to pick our way amongst those rocky things, but we can see to do that. It won't be a caution to what we've come over already so far."

"John," he said, the tiredest and saddest he'd made himself sound so far, "I told you I didn't recognize that enchanted grove we conquered somehow. But I do know those rocks, and I know what we were told lurked there."

"Lurk?" I repeated him. "That means hide, is that right?"

"Yes, that's right. I was never allowed to go as far as that interesting rock arrangement when I was a boy."

He sat down, Indian fashion, on his moccasin heels.

"You sit down, too, and catch your breath," he said. "I'm going to have to explain to you about the Raven Mockers."

XII

That's what Reuben Manco said: the Raven Mockers.

I'd heard the name of them before that, one-two times from Reuben Manco his own self and a couple times more from other old Cherokee fellows I've known well enough for them to talk to me about it. Maybe it sounds foolish to put all these things out and say I never once had aught of a notion they weren't gospel truth. But after what had already gone with us, that hard, far way up Wolter Mountain in the night, to hear Reuben Manco's talk was like to hear somebody's talk in your dream. Because whatever's said in a dream, air word and air sentence sounds like the true gospel truth. You're in the world of that dream where things are different from when you're awake.

He explained me things about the Raven Mocker belief while we sat there together, and later on when the business was all over and done with he filled me in a heap more about them. By that later time I'd had me a plenty of good reasons to believe. And here today, I reckon folks in general should ought to know what the Raven Mockers are, and what they can fix to do to you.

The way he told me about it then, they're one of the things the old-time Cherokees call *anisgina*, a name they use that means different kinds of pure down bad creatures. It doesn't mean only the ghosts of dead folks a-using round to get into mischief, but likewise other sorts of things that aren't ghosts exactly, but aren't a natural kind of thing either. Evil spirits, I should reckon, is like enough as good as a word as you can say for it in the American language.

Amongst those *anisgina* things, I should offer that the Raven Mockers can be put down for near about the worst of all. They were given that name because they can fly if they want to, and when they fly, they make a noise like a raven. Reuben Manco imitated it for me, *kraa-kraa,* a pure down ugly noise. They make it their chief business to help a man to die, you might could say. If somebody gets down flat on his back, bad sick or wounded, the Raven Mockers fly in and crowd all round and over him like a bunch of, well, like ravens. Most times they make themselves right hard to see by air real man or woman except maybe a wise old Cherokee medicine man. And the medicine man has got to pray his strongest prayers and work his best and fastest and sensiblest with all the magic he knows, so as to keep those Raven Mockers off from the one they're out to kill.

Because they're a-fixing to suck out his life, suck the very blood out of his heart. I've heard tell some such tale about another sort of things in the countries of the Old World. Only folks from over yonder call them vampires, and their voices shake just to say the name.

Raven Mockers can make themselves seen or unseen whichever they like. They can even pass themselves off to be just ordinary folks. Another time than when we were up there on that mountain, Reuben Manco narrated to me about a Cherokee hunter who was a-following a deer on a lone trail through some woods and came up on what he reckoned was just a stranger man and his wife, a-sitting in their camp. He sat down with them, the friendly way Indians can have with other Indians, and he thought they were all right till he made out what they had a-cooking on a green twig over a fire, to eat for their dinner. It was a human heart. So then, he quick got right up and took on out of there fast as he could run, and right glad he was that he got away and lived to tell of it.

But what Reuben Manco gave me while we sat together in the light on the moon was just only his main rundown of the facts on the Raven Mockers. For they were what he purely expected we'd run smack into if we kept on a-going that way we'd taken.

Anyhow, we'd have to keep on a-going, or else turn back and know inside ourselves that we deserved the name of cowards forever. It was one or the other. But as I sat on the rocks and heard his talk, I had it in mind that all those promised perils we'd met and found our way through weren't perils any great much, not compared to what seemed to be a-hanging round to wait for us up ahead.

When Reuben Manco was done with what he'd taken the time to tell me, we both stood up again and kind of stretched.

"Brother John," he said, "did you ever stop and meditate, what trouble you can get into when you're being unselfish?"

"I reckon that thing can be truly said, Chief," I replied him. "But I also reckon that no selfish fellow gets it one tad easier or happier in life than the unselfish ones."

"We won't quarrel about that," he grinned. "And forgive me for wondering if you were sorry about this project of ours."

He and I drank another mouthful of water each, and there was just a little small bit of it left to slosh inside his canteen. Then we studied all those rocks up ahead of us.

They stood a-waiting there yonder, clumped up together in the night. They were sort of like a settlement of houses, I thought, only no windows to have lights in them. Some of them were big-house size, and back in the midst of them was stuck up a sort of rocky finger, like a crooked steeple for a church. It didn't go straight up in the air like a sure-enough steeple. It angled off to the side, all black and secret and knobbed, and it looked to be a-pointing toward a blazing star near where that full moon hung so pale.

"Hold on a moment before we go closer," said Reuben Manco. "Here, right here beside us, is what I hope can bring us some good luck."

I gopped down at the brushy clump his finger pointed out to me.

"Shoo," I said, "that looks to be just only some cedar scrub."

"That's exactly what it is," he agreed me. "And cedar has always been a particularly good medicine tree for us Cherokees, because it's a bad medicine tree for all kinds of *anisgina*."

He went close to the clump and bent himself down and twisted off green, leafy twigs from it. He crushed them hard betwixt his hands and then rubbed the juice of them on his face. "Do as I do, John," he bade me. "This may be the very help we need."

So I laid down my ash stick and pulled myself some little branches of cedar. Their hard green needles mashed up when I pressed them in my hands. I laid them up against my face and rubbed them there, the way he'd done. They stung where they came to the cut on my cheek. The smell of them was sharp and right good.

"Use more," he kept a-telling me. "Use plenty of them. Rub them on your neck, that's what the enemy strikes for. Yes, and up and down your arms, too, and wherever else your skin is exposed."

Then he started in to sing under his breath. Likely it

was the same prayer song he'd hummed and crooned over those pieces of ash tree we had.

I'd have sung that song if I'd known it, but, not knowing it, I kept still. Otherwise I did the same thing he'd done, I dabbed those cedar leaves all over me where I showed out of my clothes. On the places the thorns had raked me, their juice smarted. Reuben Manco kept on a-breaking off more little branches, and he stuck them into his belt all the way round. I copied that, too, and I shoved others down inside the high tops of my shoes and drew up the laces as tight as I could, so as to hold them there. We both chewed up some tags of the cedar. They were tangy sharp on my tongue, made a good taste there. And I poked a big green cedar twig into the ring that held the elephant charm to the thong round my neck.

Reuben Manco showed me how to rub yet more cedar all over the length of my ash stick from one end to the other. After that, he gathered near about all the branches we'd left on the clump. They made a good armful, and he took a string from his pocket and tied them together. He ran his arm through the loop and slung the whole bundle to his elbow.

"That place up ahead has always been described to me as being as much like hell as possible," he said, calm and quiet. "Do you believe in hell, John?"

"I reckon I do believe in hell," I replied him, "and I'll wager you it's so full of sinners that their feet stick out the windows."

He laughed at that, a truly happy-sounding laugh. "I believe in it too," he told me. "I've seen too many outlying precincts of it lately for me to be skeptical."

He hiked up his bundle of cedar again.

"All right," he said, "we're probably as ready to go ahead there as we can possibly manage."

Side by side, we made ourselves walk toward that big

old clutter of rocks where, he'd said, trouble was right likely to be a-waiting for us.

The light right then and there was more or less about what I'd have expected to find on the moon itself, up yonder sometime when you could see things by what was reflected from off the sun by the Earth; Earthshine, I reckon is the best thing to call it. Where the rocks stood huddled in that light, they looked all softly gleamy, but another sight less than as gleamy as the moon was. In the shadows that lay down amongst them, things were as deep black as if they'd been painted over there with tar.

And one thing I could feel right off, that stretch of the rock of the mountain down under our feet was plumb bare and solid and bald. No ferns or tufty grass, nor yet even moss, grew there. The last growing stuff we'd come across was that one scrubby bunch of cedar, back yonder. In air place else, it was like as if somebody had come along with a chunk of fire and burned off each single scrap of growing thing that otherwise might be there, might be popped up here and yonder betwixt the rocks. Time and again since that night, I've wondered myself if that was what had happened, if there'd been truly some kind of burn-off there, for one reason or another.

Our two pairs of feet, his in moccasins, mine in shoes, made little clinky sounds on the face of that dry rock as we made ourselves walk closer, closer. On there ahead, the big clutter of boulders looked more like a bunch of houses than before, and now I could make out what looked like a dark alleyway in amongst them.

That put one more creepy feeling into my mind, as I kept a-tramping along, one foot in front of the other. Those big house-shaped chunks of stone had to be just chunks of stone, I lectured to myself. There wasn't air point in imagining that they had roofs and walls to them.

And naturally there couldn't be windows, not anyway toward us as we closed in. But what if there were windows, and, all of a sudden quick, something or other lighted a lamp in one of them? I shook my head, hard, to get shed of that ugly fancy, but somehow it didn't seem to shake out.

"Come ahead, John," Reuben Manco half whispered to me, though he didn't have the need to tell me that. I was a-coming ahead, all right, with that stout old chunk of ash tree clamped tight in my right fist.

By then, we'd brought ourselves along right close to the first big rock beside where the black alleyway-place opened and took itself in beyond. That rock was house-size, all right. If it had been a sure enough house, it would have been a good comfortable size for a family of, say, four. It was tall enough for two stories, and up at the top it rose like the peak of a roof. I'd come near enough to it to make out that its side looked to be how a rock is that's been split off from another chunk of the same stuff. It hadn't been left right smooth, but not right rough, either. You can see pieces of slate broken off like that, pieces of shale broken off like that. Broken granite or limestone is more rough and jaggly and all mommicked up to the look. I reckoned that, by bright sunlight, that house-shaped rock would be a pale brown. But by that light of the moon, it was more tawny than pale. And it had that sneaky look of a house, so much so that I wondered right out loud, "Why in hell doesn't it have windows?"

"I can't help but ask myself the same question," said Reuben Manco's soft voice alongside me. "I can feel myself being looked at."

And that was what, that feeling of something a-looking at us. The way it had been down below on the Forshay place when we'd had that notion of spies a-using all round about us here and there. Only up on that mountain, it was a right much stronger feeling.

Did you ever have to march down the street in a parade, with a whole slew of folks all pushed up together along the curbs and a-giving you the eye? You can feel the weight of their eyes when that happens, and I felt it right then and there, high up on those rocks in the light of the moon, as Reuben Manco and I passed along close to that big house-looking chunk and pointed ourselves to go into the dark passageway where God and all the angels knew what might could be a-waiting there to tole us in.

For about a second's time I did think there was a window up in the rock, after all, though likely it was only a flicker in the moonlight on one place of it. Reuben stopped at the mouth of the dark open place and tried his best to see into it. After a moment he started on in, with his stick held out in front of him to feel the way along, like a blind man with a cane. I made myself follow in back of him. In the moonless alley, he was only just a black blob there a-moving in front of me. I knew that the rocks made high walls to the two sides of us; rocks as dark as inside a cave, and with no windows in them, either.

My shoes made echoes in there, echoes that growled. Reuben Manco's moccasins just shuffled on their way. And there, too, we could hear those ghosts of voices, but not quite the same voices that had seemed to speak to us at those other creepy places. These said something like *oooh oooh,* so pure down sort and sad you had to strain with your ears to hear it. *Oooh oooh,* they said to us, like as if they tried to answer the sounds of our feet. I wondered myself what it was they were a-trying to say to us, was it good or bad.

The passage wound and wound betwixt the tall rocks, this-a-way and that-a-way. Time and time again, we bumped into those rocks as we groped ourselves along. It was that plumb hard to see where to go. At last, before we knew that we'd come to it, we found ourselves out in the open, where a soft wash of light shed itself down.

There was a space amongst the rocks that had shoved all round us. I felt there was something up overhead, it might could be even a growth of some kind, though we hadn't seen air growth in air place, all along the way past the cedar scrub. Maybe it was just some more rocks up there above us, opened out with cracks betwixt them to filter down enough light for us to see by a little. And what we saw there didn't comfort us, not one bit at all.

Because, over yonder to one side, in an angle of two split-apart rocks, there stood a skeleton. It was as pale as cream and as silent as the stones themselves, a-seeming to look on us with those shadowy eyeholes in its bare skull.

I recollect that I said something I wouldn't want written down for my last words on this Earth. I hiked up my old ash stick, ready to hit out with it if I had to. But Reuben Manco took it easier anyhow.

"When somebody shows us that many naked bones, he's past being dangerous," he muttered to me, and it was good to think that.

He craned his neck to look all round the open space. It was as big as a big yard in there. The bottom of it was as hard as a paved floor, and the rocky sides rose up high all round us, with starry sky far up above. As we stood there to look, I thought that there were things a-sliding over us in the air. Not bats. They were another sight too big for bats. The flew back and forth, too fast for us to get a good look at them. Maybe I wouldn't have much relished a-having a good look at them.

Meanwhile, Reuben Manco walked, slow and steady, toward that skeleton stood up in the split corner of the wall. After just a second, I walked there likewise.

"Nothing to fear," said Reuben Manco, a-talking quietly as he always did. "It's just a set of human bones. Perfectly articulated. It was deliberately set up there, as you can see. Undoubtedly somebody died here, and his flesh is gone."

I gave it a study, close up.

"Look, Chief, it's been fastened to the rock," I pointed out. "Looky there, it was chained in place."

That was a fact. Round where its waist had been, where naught remained except the knobby backbone, a ring of links held it up against the rock so it wouldn't fall. I could see the lean bones that had been the hands. They were joined in front. The bony fingers were twined together, the way you hold your hands to say a prayer.

"And he was spiked through the head," said Reuben Manco.

That was the truth, too. A big, rough, black-looking spike had been driven right betwixt the empty eyes, and into the rock beyond. I came closer to look at it.

"It's iron," said Reuben Manco. "Eaten with rust."

"I judge that his folks have given up a-waiting for him to come back home."

"The spike through the head was a ceremonial business with the ancient Druids," said Reuben Manco, very softly. "Well, whoever he was, he died an ugly death. And so did his companion there just at his feet.

I stooped and saw what he'd made out in the darkness at floor level. More bones there, laid flat and fallen apart, beside the standing skeleton.

"Two of them," said Reuben Manco.

And two of us, I thought. We'd have to look sharp if we didn't want to be left as bones our own selves.

"How do you reckon they got killed here?" I wondered us.

"They must have come for what they thought was a good purpose, John. The way we have come. It's an extremely bad place to come."

Again he studied those two sets of bones, all over.

"I don't see any sure evidence of any violence, though of course it may have happened just to their flesh. Well, but theorizing seldom helps very much. Let's keep going along."

We could make out, just barely, where the alleyway went on beyond to another open space. It looked even darker and narrower, the alley, than where we'd first gone into it. Reuben Manco reached out with his stick and felt his way in, and again I followed along on his heels. As I did that, one of the flying things swooped down close to our heads, and I thought I could see its eyes like soft sparks. Then it was gone away somewhere, out of sight again.

I puzzled myself about the Raven Mockers he'd told me those things about. It stands to reason, tales of such a sort come down from something that was real, or anyway had been real one time. I recollected all that talk with Holly and Luke at the Forshay cabin about old, old kinds of men, or you might could call them just half-men, that the science folks thought had been in America all those long-ago ages back yonder. Half-man things would naturally hate true men; maybe because they were too close the same in some ways, too far apart in others. I tried to study what it had been like in those early times, with wars betwixt men and half-men. They would have had to be pure down terrible wars, fought till one side or the other won. I'd been in a war myself, and, gentlemen, that had been terrible enough. War is hateful. Too bad that's how we go about to settle things.

This part of the alleyway was narrower than the first part, as I said. And it was another sight darker, too. I figured maybe the rock had closed itself clean over, above our heads. We walked single file in that choking blackness, me behind Reuben Manco. I could feel one wall with my stick and the other one with my hand. I heard our feet when they made more echoes in there. Or was something a-moving along with us? No telling, not for sure anyway. I wonder myself now if I wished I could be sure.

We came out again into more open space, stretched out far wider than the last one, and the moon glowed down to show it to us there. High walls of rock all the way round, but this time they weren't solid. They had caves in them, each one as black as the night of judgment day. A whole long string of caves, all the way this and that. Softly, softly as something you can barely remember, softly as the sound of water far, far off, I heard *oooh oooh oooh*, soft and sad. And I wished to heaven it wouldn't make itself heard.

In the middle of the rocky open space there lay water. I could make out the shine and flicker of it in the light of the moon and the stars. First off, I couldn't give the least notion of a guess how deep it lay, nor yet if it stirred with some kind of current to it. But it was big enough for a big swimming pool, if some strange creature or other felt like a-going in for a dip.

And at its edge stood the first tree I'd seen since we'd cut the cedar branches back yonder. It wasn't a tree much bigger than a tall bush, and right there in the month of June it didn't have air single leaf a-growing on it. It's branches clawed out their naked twigs like the prongs on the antlers of a big buck deer. I near about expected it to toss those antler-branches.

Reuben Manco wasn't a-looking at the tree, not right then. "I can see a way out for us on the far side, just over there," he said to me, and he let his voice sound happy to say it.

But right when he spoke was when the soft *oooh oooh* turned all of a sudden to a loud, nasty *kraa-kraa-kraa*, all over the place. And things came a-stealing out, on all sides of us, from those dark caves every which-a-way in the moonlight.

XIII

Gentlemen, how can my poor tongue tell you what those things looked like? How can I tell you aught about them unless I try to say how they looked?

Naturally, I didn't see them plain, not right off when they were a-coming out of their dark places into the moonlight, to slide into a sort of circle round us. My first thought was, they were dark and sort of secret—they stood up but they weren't right tall. Maybe five feet or so, for the most part. They looked to be draped and folded round about, like as if they had on cloaks or blankets, like the old-timey Indians. Their heads were round and dark, with a knobby look all over them, and the heads and those wrappings were the same sooty-looking color that, in the sunlight, might could have been a deep, dirty brown. They'd come on out and spread this-a-way and that to surround us, and they stood and looked on us with eyes like coals of fire that had died down to a scummy pink.

"Stand back to back with me, John," said Reuben Manco, calm and quiet and steady, the way he'd talked from the first of things. "Stand and face them on your side and I'll face them on mine."

I felt him brush against my shoulder as he moved on round behind me. I did what he said to do. I faced my side of that circle.

In that much of the surround I could see, one of them came on a little out from amongst the close bunch of its fellows. I don't truly reckon it was air much different from the others, saving that it was a shade bigger perhaps, but it acted like a leader amongst them. It came on a couple-three steps, stiffy-legged, toward me. I could look on it and see it, plainer than I could see the whole pack of them at the one time.

Right off, it put me in mind of something. Its face looked like a mask, but it wasn't. That was its sure-enough face. What showed of its darkness when the moon came down on it, was like those rocks up off the way to the Forshay spring on the mountain trail. And enough like a mask that you'd wonder yourself why it didn't take the mask off. Only no such thing. It wouldn't have come off.

It had that monkeyish look to it, only not just monkey, either. Monkeys are funny, and this wasn't funny. I mean, the skull was squashed low and shallow above and its jaw was wide and shallow below. Its mouth hung loose and ugly and went all the way across, and its two pink-shining eyes hung deep back in it, in hollows like pits under two big bony brows like jackknife handles. But not funny like a monkey, or either with that sad monkey look. It was pure poison mean. And, I reckoned, hungry.

For a second there, face to face with it, I told myself we'd been gumps not to fetch along those guns Creed Forshay had wanted us to take at his place. But in the same second I likewise told myself that a gun wouldn't be air good whatsoever against such a thing as that, not the biggest gun a man could tote along with him.

Meanwhile, I stood there and saw it, and it sure enough saw me. It gave me a good stare with its glowing eyes, the way it might be a-trying to figure out some way to get a hold of me. I grabbed tighter hold on my ash club.

All through the rest of the close-standing bunch behind

that one I could hear that sigh of sound, *oooh oooh*, like as if I was a-being mourned for without my being done for yet. But the one who had stepped out there in front of me made nair sound whatsoever. It stood, and then it took one more stiff step on what must have been short legs and big, lumpy feet. Its coals of eyes glinted at me.

"Just stand steady, John," said Reuben Manco next to my ear. "I think they're a trifle afraid to close in if we face them."

I couldn't reckon what might could be a-going on, that side where we stood his watch. But one, at least, of that dark, ugly crowd was a-trying to set itself to close in on me. It stirred another slow step closer, and the drapes of dark stuff round it opened up.

And then I could see it wasn't a-wearing a cloak or blanket, nothing of the sort. No kind of clothes at all. For the long, jointy arms spread out to either side. And the drape spread out with them and stretched from them. It was grown to them. It was part of them.

I could see a dimness of the moon's bright light that soaked through that stretched-out stuff. That stuff was a kind of skin. It grew downward from the wrists and elbows of the long arms, it was fast to the two sides of the squatty body, all the way down to the ankles of the short, chunky legs. It was like the spread of an umbrella, or of the wings of a bat. Only it had no ribs to it, just the wide-pulled stretch of it you could see the moonlight through.

Right at that moment was when I told myself for sure that these things must be the Raven Mockers I'd heard tell about from Reuben Manco.

I don't rightly know today whether I was scared at that time. A thing can come along and happen to you, and you don't have the time to make up your mind if you're scared, because there's so almighty much else you've got to tend to somehow. Right then, I seemed to tell myself that if these were the Raven Mockers, I was plumb lucky that one of them had moved out to be ahead of the others. Because that-a-way, it had made itself some sort of leader. And if there's a bunch of anything against you, pick out just one of them to be the leader and try to settle things with that one. The others just might could wait back and watch instead of a-ganging up on you.

When I made up my mind to that, I decided to say something.

"All right," I told that Raven Mocker who had stepped out to me, "I don't rightly know if you're the meanest one in this crowd, but I reckon you're sure God the ugliest. Nobody can deny you that."

It stood there and seemed to hear me, and it winnowed those wing-skins wider. I studied that maybe it wanted to wrap me up in them. With the wing-things spread out tight on the arms, I could make out that it had hands, too, held open. The fingers were long and knobby-jointed, like stalks of dry cane. They had the meanest-looking of claws spread out at their tips. Its head tilted to one side, and I had a better look at the monkey face. Its brows were pulled together into a frown, the mouth stretched into a grin, and in the mouth were great big teeth, ragged and stale-looking in a ray of the moon. It was as ugly-looking a face as I've said.

Back to back with me, Reuben Manco mumbled words in his Cherokee talk. Prayers, I made no doubt. I wondered if one of the Raven Mockers yonder was a-making a move toward him, too, but I didn't dare look back to find out. I had my own business to tend to, right there in front of me.

"All right, come on," I dared that one who'd dared me. "Come ahead, and don't stop and tarry by the way. You're a-looking for trouble, and I've got a good lavish plenty of it for you, right here and now."

I hefted my stout ash club a little more than waist high in front of me. I grinned my own teeth at the Raven Mocker, though well I knew they didn't look so deadly hungry as its teeth. I moved my feet a little apart, the right one forward, to stand more solid and ready.

Another windy flap of its spread wing-skins, and it came a-squattering in at me.

All the others sighed out *oooh* when it made its move. I saw it open its wing-things all the way to fling them round me. Then I slid my right foot in toward it and made a swing with my club. It slammed right straight in at the Raven Mocker's knobby dark head, but it didn't hit against aught that was rightly solid. It felt the way it would have felt if I'd smacked it into fast-flowing water, it bobbed in my hand was all. But, solid whack or not, the Raven Mocker went back into a stumble. I saw it near about fall down. It flapped the wing-things to stay on its feet or hind paws or whatever you want to call them. It hollered out *kraa-kraa,* and well I knew that it could be hurt and that I'd hurt it. The whole circle of the others moaned *oooh* all together, and to me they sounded bothered.

The one I'd hit that hard lick just tottered and scraped with its feet to grab hold of the ground under them. A man would have gone flat down under a whack like that, but the Raven Mocker was no man, was nothing to be fought like a man. It got itself steady and came a-stumping in toward me again, with its wings spread. I jabbed at it with the end of my club, hard as I could jab.

Like before, I didn't hit a solid thing, no more than I'd seemed to hit aught real when I slammed down at its head. The ash wood just drove and sank on through whatever that ugly dark body was, went right on through like through a bucket of slush. I almost stumbled down on my face. I felt the wing-skins as they brushed in to try to wrap round me, and I got a whiff of smell like from a snake den, but I straightened myself up away and out of reach from them. Next moment, the Raven Mocker had stiff-legged on back away from me, three-four shaky steps, and the other behind it gave back a little too.

Kraa-kraa-kraa, all of them made their hellacious ear-hurting noise together. Some of them had sort of climbed their way up in the air, a-beating their wing-skins to flop and flutter clear from the ground. I tried to crowd my back up against Reuben Manco's, but I couldn't find him there to crowd to. He had gone away from behind me.

"Chief!" I hollered out my loudest, and swung my head round to look for what had gone with him, my eyes off from the ones at my own side.

Then's when they all rushed me, and quick I hit again, before they were close in enough to do their own hitting. I felt the flap of their wing-skins. One of them scraped my face. It had that sickly snaky smell, it felt sweaty and dirty. They were all a-trying to grab onto me, swaddle me up, maybe shut off my breath. I fought back at them and only half-felt them, it was like a swim in the almightiest nasty water in the world. One had its claws a-driving at my throat, but it snatched them quick back away with a *kraa-kraa* howl that all but deafened my ears. That loud racket made the rest of them pull off away, and I wiggled myself out from amongst them. The cedar, or that good ash pole, or the elephant charm slung round my neck, or likely all three—they'd helped me get away right then.

"Chief!" I yelled again.

Then I saw where he'd gone off to. He'd likewise pulled himself clear somehow, had broken his way out through that dark, flopping crowd. He'd made a run like a rabbit toward the pool yonder at the center of the open space, with all the stars a-hanging down overhead like ripe shiny fruits about to drop. I saw him, all stooped over by that naked tree with its bare twiggy branches like deerhorns above him.

That very same moment I saw him, the whole bunch of the Raven Mockers wheeled itself around, and I reckon they all saw him, too. One and all, they started to stumble that-a-way to get after him again.

But Reuben Manco had quick grabbed him up a scatter of twigs from under the tree, and he'd struck fire right against the roots. I reckon he must have used one of those flip-on pipe lighters. I saw a finger of flame blaze itself up, and then he had gone down on one knee beside it, a-doing something or other I couldn't make out. Up came vapory curls of smoke, full of sparks, from that fire he'd set there.

The Raven Mockers all sighed out together at that, miserable and creepy-sounding with their awful voices. They sort of teetered on their lumps of feet and flapped up and down with their wing-skins. Just right then, they weren't a-pushing close round me. So I up and ran like hell and got myself to where Reuben Manco was.

The tree had burst up all a climbing blaze of fire. Its wood must have been as dry as a twist of hay. I saw the hot flames as they jumped and scrambled up into those antlery branches, a-making each twig burn like a candle. The flames made red, bright dances of glow on the rocks round about, and on the water. Reuben Manco swung himself round to face me. His face flickered in the firelight.

"Here, John, use this," he said.

He shoved something at me and I took it. It was a bunch of those cedar twigs he'd fetched along, all wrung tight round one another and set afire at one end. I got a tangy whiff of the smoke. "Use that against them," he said, and lifted up another burning twist in his own hand.

I made a quick turn round on my boot heel, under the trembling light from that burning tree. The Raven Mockers had come to group themselves round us again, but this time they hung back off. One held up his wing-skin like a cloak to hide his monkey face from the light and smoke. I saw their eyes sort of shimmer, saw the jaggy teeth in their open mouths. I waited for them to try a rush at us. But they didn't rush. They stood where they were, with their big ugly mouths gopped open.

"Easy, John," said Reuben Manco. "We'll make our own approach march this time."

Slow as slow but steady as steady, he made a step forward. Another step, more steps. He carried his cedar torch held up high over his head, his ash stick low and ready at his side in the other hand. I kept along with him. He waved his torch and it gave off a swirl of bright, hot sparks. In front of him, the dark line bowed back in a waver.

By God, they acted scared of us.

"I think it's going to work," said Reuben Manco, barely loud enough for me to hear the words.

We kept a-walking on toward them, and they kept on their way back, not fast, but on the move. I recollected what Reuben Manco had allowed to me about the power of cedar smoke with such things as that. It appeared like as if they just couldn't much stand up to the smell of its burning that-a-way.

Reuben Manco swung his torch back and forth across him from left to right, as far as his arm would go both ways. More sparks danced up from the burning cedar. The braids of his hair danced on his shoulders. The light flickered in and out on those big, staring faces, dark and monkeyfied, and the fire-coal eyes in the faces blinked off as they turned themselves away. I swung my torch, too, while we walked toward them. We walked close. That part of the line we walked at gave back from us, and back, the two ends not moving as fast as the middle. The line made a bow away from us. The wing-skins fluttered in it, the faces bobbed and scrunched and turned away.

"Swing your fire around and around, John," Reuben Manco told me. "We don't want any of them closing in and getting behind us."

I whirled my torch round my head. It stirred the air and made the fire blaze up and crackle. I heard *oooh* as the ones in front backed away from the cedar smoke that smelled so sharp and strong in the air. They weren't about to wait for us to come to them.

"Straight ahead," said Reuben Manco, a-going straight ahead his own self.

And I said inside myself, if this sort of night had to be passed up on this mountaintop so full of what shouldn't ought to have ever been, I sure enough had the right sort of friend along with me. For he was a medicine man of the Cherokees, the tribe that was called one of the Civilized Nations, but which hadn't purely given up all of its old, old ways and knowledges just to be civilized. Now Reuben Manco was half-whispering, half-singing again in his Cherokee language. It must have been another song to drive bad medicine away, drive it before him. The way it was the other times, I didn't know enough Cherokee to join in with him. So all I could do was whisper my own prayer under my breath.

What I said was the Twenty-third Psalm, *Though I walk through the Valley of the Shadow of Death, I shall fear no evil*. Not that I didn't fear the evil there where we walked, there where Death flung his shadow on us, hungry for us, killing mad at us. But if I feared it, I faced up to it anyway. A man's got to be a man sometime. You show me one who was nair afraid, and I'll right away show you one that nair in his life came up against aught to fear.

We'd headed ourselves at the center of the line, I say. *Oooh,* they moaned, and they opened out and off from one another, and we were a-going through the empty space. We whirled our torches all the time. I wondered how long the burning cedar would last. And then we'd come clean through, out to the other side of their open line, and I looked back as I went.

The Raven Mockers had bunched up together again. Two-three of them rose in the air, a-flopping those ugly wing-skins. They looked like floating kites, but I'd have hated to know the boy who'd care to fly such a looking kite. Reuben Manco kept on a-slogging ahead. He pointed himself for where there showed a gap in the rocky wall round the place, and the moon shone down into that gap.

"We've daunted them, John," he said, and went back to his song.

I hoped to heaven that he said the truth. I looked back one more time. Sure enough, they'd started to move after us again, but they didn't try to push at all close.

"Mind your feet, John," said Reuben Manco. "Mind your feet, don't stumble, and don't be afraid. Because there never was a better time not to be afraid."

In front of us, something moved and squirmed on the bare earth. I felt air hair on my head stand up, for it was like the biggest snake you could see in your worst bad dream. But it was fast to the ground at one end, like a big old root a-coming up out of there, only no tree or bush or aught else that it might could be rooted to. It sort of slithered toward us where we walked. Reuben Manco stopped in his tracks, and when its small end whipped toward him, he jumped high and over it and ran a few steps out on the other side. Next moment, I'd jumped over it, too, and I ran, and I felt my heart go thumpetty-bang inside me. Reuben Manco had slowed to a walk again.

"We're all right now, it's fast to the ground," he said, in that same calm voice of his.

"What is it, Chief?"

"No time to tell you just now, but the old Cherokees had legends about such things. Don't worry, we're leaving it behind us."

But the Raven Mockers followed, a good piece back.

We were a-coming to the gap. On both sides of it rose the rocks, with big chunks on top of them, set the way you'd think they were ready to fall down air moment. But we went on through. It wasn't a long ways through, nor near as dark as the way in had been.

All of a sudden, I felt some better again. For we'd come out yonder on the far side of the rock wall, with trees a-growing in front of us, and the moon almost straight up in the sky overhead. The stars still stared down on us, but not quite so much like the eyes of the Raven Mockers. I looked into those dark trees.

"Right off, I think it looks sort of familiar just here," I allowed to Reuben Manco. "I've got it in mind that, in through these trees a little small way, is where we come to the Forshay spring and those funny-looking rocks, and the trail to the Voth place forks off there."

"You make me glad to hear we're that close," he said back to me. "Because it must be nearly midnight, and midnight on this day of the year, under the full moon, is the time for the principal Druidic sacrificial ceremony to begin."

I looked up yonder to the pale bonfire of the moon, and

all at once I saw that clouds were on their way up to it. On their way all round the sky from above the trees, a-climbing, a-climbing, heavy and dark as the flow of a muddy winter pond.

We picked up our feet and started our walk toward that patch of trees I reckoned I knew.

Oh yes, I thought to myself, and I've done a sight of walking in right rough dangerous places tonight, done it by the mountain man's two-foot rule—two feet and a long step betwixt them. When could I stop and rest? Not now, anyway.

"We were lucky back yonder," I said.

"We were ready, we were able to stand them off," he replied me. "We weren't off guard, like Mr. Forshay was when he was knocked down and his son and Holly were captured."

"You think that those were Raven Mockers at the cabin?"

"Probably. Seven perils in our way, and I conjecture that those Raven Mockers we just got away from were the sixth of them."

I ran things over in my mind as I walked.

"Six, that's right, Chief," I said. "The boar pig. That near-about fall off the cliff. That foggy patch. The fiery place where we pole-vaulted over, and then that grove of ash and oak and thorn." I nodded my head for each one. "And sixth was back in yonder, where a couple of times I wondered myself it we wouldn't be stopped."

"Neither of us was exactly ready to be stopped," he said. "You're a tall, strong man in your prime, and I'm still a going concern at my age. Raven Mockers are mostly deadly to those who are weak or sick or wounded."

"They sure enough wanted us," I said, my eyes on the trees we were headed for.

"But we stood them off. They were the sixth peril, if I'm not getting boresomely repetitious. Which leaves us one more."

In the smoky-dark clouds over the trees, a fork of lightning crackled for just a second. We walked. My feet were heavy in my boots. I'd got myself plumb worn down with all this we'd been through.

"What do you reckon the seventh peril will be?" I asked.

"Without trying to be arbitrary, I wonder if it won't be those Voth brothers themselves. And the god they worship."

XIV

I took a quick, hard look at that wise old Indian, and he looked back at me, with the pale light a-soaking down on us.

"Whatever god?" I repeated him, and it must have sounded as dumb as most repeated things do, for he laughed a soft laugh.

"Baal," replied Reuben Manco. "I've told you about Baal, the chief god of the Druids. Of the same name as the god of the Babylonians and the Assyrians, and the Philistines in the Bible. He's not so widely remembered these days, Brother John, not by the world at large. About all we can be sure of from those old stone images, is that he had a beard."

He was a-grinning to himself about that, I couldn't for sure tell why.

"He had a beard," he said again. "It would appear that beards usually go with gods among ancient peoples of the Old World. Zeus had a fine, curly one. Wotan had a beard, and so did Thor. So did the Baals in Babylon and Assyria, and before them in places like Akkad and Elam— big spade beards, carved out of immemorial stone. And how about the god you were brought up to worship, John, doesn't he have a beard, too?"

"Why," I said, while we tramped along, "come to think of that, I used to always kind of reckon he did."

"Of course your white man's god has a beard," said

Reuben Manco. "Look at the portrait Michelangelo painted to identify him, in the Sistine Chapel. But," and he grinned that grin another time, "the Indians never saw a beard on God, whatever they decided to name him."

In the moonlight he put up his hand to his brown cheek, where no beard grew.

"Never with us Cherokees," he said, "and never with the Algonquins who called him Manitou, nor yet with the Sioux who called him Watonka. Not yet with Huitzilo-pochtli of the Aztecs, nor Pachacamac of the Peruvians." He kept on a-grinning and a-patting his wise, brown face. "So, my brother, perhaps I'm not obligated to fear a god with a beard. Anyway, I'm not going to fear Baal. Come on, let's find out what he amounts to."

He picked up his moccasined feet on the way to the trees. I went along beside him. It's right hard to say just what way his talk made me feel better, feel more like a-getting at things and a-winding up this business right, but it did. It came to mind that I was smooth-shaven my own self. I wondered would it help us. I sure enough hoped my best that it would.

Not that I was too smooth in the face at that, it struck me as I walked toward those trees I felt I knew. It was getting on to midnight, and I'd been up right soon that morning, near about eighteen hours back, and had shaved at the Forshay cabin. I put my memory back over the doings of the day, and there'd been a right much of stuff to happen to all folks concerned in them. I could even remember what we'd had to eat. Eggs and all like that for breakfast, then Luke and I had gone to Sky Notch to get Holly Christopher and fetch her back. And for noon dinner, peanut butter sandwiches along with all the talk. After that, Holly and I had gone to find Reuben Manco and beg to him to help us. Reuben Manco's good venison stew for supper. And betwixt all those things, the magic we'd made out to do, out where the cross thing from up at the spring was buried and spoken over, then in the cabin the spell against those spying eyes of whatever they were in the heads of. And Holly and me, a-going up the trail to visit the Voths in their hellacious house.

All those things had been strange and scary, here and there. But other different things had been a-going on. Holly and Luke had started out to act like fond lovers, even that short day together. And Reuben Manco and I, we'd found out that we were like brothers, and he said that word to me, called me Brother John. Yes indeed, gentlemen, enough stuff had gone on betwixt sunrise and midnight to last the ordinary sort of folks a month.

"How much time have we got, Chief?" I asked.

"Time enough, Brother John. Just about time enough, as I estimate. I don't think it's any too much time."

"We're getting right close to where I'll know the way in."

"And I'm delighted to hear you say so."

Another flash of lightning on high, that squirmed over us like a fiery crawling snake, and a sort of drummy roll of thunder. Weather was a-getting ready to happen. We tramped our way along to the trees, and we got to them. I felt my way in shadows to where the land banked down.

"Here we are," I said to Reuben Manco, and swung myself over the bank and landed on my feet on the trail below. Next moment, he came down, too.

Sure enough, there was the spring that gave water to the Forshay place. We could hear its ripply voice in the darkness of the cave where it came up. I tried to look down along the trail that led slanting on the ledge of Wolter Mountain. I couldn't see it at all plain, but I knew it was there. All of a sudden quick, I felt better, like as if new blood pumped into my tired body. After those perils in places strange to me, I was on ground I'd been on before, I could be sure of where my feet stood.

"And now," I said, "just along here a tad. Here, Chief, we're at where those stones make their figures by the trail. Over across them and beyond, and we're on the way to the Voth house."

Reuben Manco had stooped himself over at the spring, to fill his canteen. He straightened up again and came along to me, a-holding the canteen out.

"Aren't you a trifle thirsty?" he said.

"I thank you," I said back, and hiked the canteen up to take me a big mouthful and slosh it all round in my throat. It cooled me, made me feel better still. Reuben Manco took him a drink, too, and screwed the cap back on the canteen and slid it back into its pouch.

"Up this way, you said," he grunted and walked on to where those stones were set on the slope.

"Hold on," I said. "Wait up. Hark at me, Chief, I know the ground beyond here. You'd better let me lead the way."

"You know the ground beyond here," he repeated me. "And also, you know the Voth brothers, and they're well acquainted with you. They'd recognize you on sight, but I'd be a stranger to them. Therefore, let me go first."

"I don't understand that talk, Chief," I tried to argue him.

"But you call me Chief, so let me give this one command." He pointed. "I'll go ahead now. You wait here until I've crossed the rocks, am out of sight. Then you come along. And wait at the top and make sure I'm out of sight on that other trail again, before you try to follow me."

"Why in hell's name do you want to be that far ahead?"

"Brother," he said, his face shoved close to mine, "you and I were both in the Army, in combat service. We both know what war means. I judge that we both have been on patrols behind enemy lines. You know how there's a getaway man assigned in a patrol, the last one on the open order march. If the enemy gets the main patrol, the last one is supposed to be missed, stays free and active. That is, if he's any good at being the getaway man."

"Don't you get to thinking that I'll be a-running away if they grab you," I sort of snarled, and he smiled.

"No, John, I don't think that at all. But I do think you'll be free and unnoticed if they have their notice concentrated on me. And you'll also do something about it. Do as I tell you, now, I'll be all right up front."

And with that, he turned and put himself to scrambling across all those rocks and boulders.

I watched him go out of sight at the top of the slope, the way he'd said for me to do, before I went up after him. I tried not to look at those image-faces amongst the rocks, they'd have put me too much in mind of the Raven Mockers. I hoped we'd left all such behind, but then I wondered myself if that might not be a vain hope.

In any case, Reuben Manco sure enough seemed to know what he was up to; though what in the name of gracious he'd be up to on that trail, the one place they'd be most bound to watch, was far and away beyond me.

I waited a second amongst brush at the top of the slope, a-looking along that trail I'd traveled the day before and the day before that. I could make it out betwixt the trees. The moonlight just barely speckled it in the places where the leaves didn't shadow it. Reuben Manco didn't show on it that I could see. I picked up my feet and followed after, the way I'd been a-following after all this long night on the mountain.

Now, there was no noise to either side of me where the

trees grew thick and brush crowded all the space amongst them. No bugs a-chirping, no tree frogs, no nothing. That surprised me some. Had maybe Reuben Manco's passing ahead shut them up? But if air living thing could move without a noise, that living thing was Reuben Manco. I looked up to where a chunk of the night sky showed through the trees. There was the same moon, like a pale shiny millstone. It had ground its way almost all the way up. I reckoned maybe a half hour's time before midnight. If that was when the Voths would do whatever they'd do to Holly and Luke, we were a-cutting it fine.

Patrol work behind enemy lines, Reuben Manco had compared it. All I'd thought about such a thing in years was that I hoped I'd nair have to do such a thing again, but here I was, a-doing it. This was enemy ground all right, this trail that belonged to the Voths. It was a wiggly trail, another sight wigglier than I'd recollected. It even seemed to wiggle as I walked it, like a walk on the back of a big old snake, a mean one that might could turn and sock its fangs into you. I set the heels of my boots down first and then the full sole, so as not to scrape on a pebble or rattle a piece of grass. I was a-moving right quietly, as quietly even as Reuben Manco his own self must be.

Anyway, I still had my good ash club. If I came up against one of the Voths, we'd find out if it wasn't just a little bitty bit harder than his head.

I came along to where the trail made a right sharp turn, with hemlocks there along the sides. I shoved up under their darkness to make the way round. As I did so, I thought that the silence was over, that I heard voices. Was that some of the way it had been time and time again, a notion of somebody a-talking? But I humped down and sneaked along under those hemlock branches, a-holding myself low so as not to rustle them. I came round the bend, and there was light up ahead where the trees came apart at the tops to let it through.

And I stopped still in my tracks.

Because, in the patch of light, I could see Reuben Manco, a-standing still on the trail. With, at the two sides of him, two things dressed up in white, gowns or robes or sheets. And a voice was a-talking to him.

Right away I dropped down on my all fours to crawl toward them, to get close enough to hear, close enough even maybe to do something.

"We have known all through the night that someone was up on this mountain where he had no business," came the voice of Brummitt Voth, clipped and ugly as homemade sin. "We knew about you all the time, every step you took on your way."

"And we're happy that you came," put in Hooper Voth's voice. "This is going to be a brilliant midsummer midnight. Three sacrifices instead of two."

Gentlemen, you can bet your neck my blood hummed at that. I kept myself from jumping up and charging. I crawled nearer, and rose up on my knee with a hemlock tree between me and them, and looked round it.

I'd come to thirty feet away from where they stood, more or less. I could see them right clear. The two Voths were draped all over in their white stuff, but they had rifles in their hands, held at the ready. Reuben Manco stood easier than they did, with his hands at his sides, as quiet as a statue of an Indian medicine man.

I wished again I had a gun too, one of those guns Creed Forshay had offered us. A repeating rifle would have been best. By that light, I could have shot one of the Voths through the head and then the other, before he could turn round to see what the shooting was about. But

without a rifle, I had to figure to do something else.
Reuben Manco had made me hang far back just in case
this might happen. What must I do?

A-thinking hard every second, I kept myself quiet and
hung back there in the thick of the hemlocks. I knew I
could do the brave thing and make a rush in yonder
where they'd captured Reuben Manco, but both of them
had guns. Such a rush as that might well be the last act I
did on this Earth, and no good to air soul in what most
likely wouldn't be the long run. I purely had to be smart
and see if I couldn't puzzle out some better way to help
Reuben Manco, get him loose, away from them. I bent
my knees a couple-three inches and held myself as quiet
as a rabbit when hunters are near by on the look for it,
and I spied out into the moonlight from that hiding place
amongst the hemlocks. Some wise old fellow told me once,
if you don't know what to do, don't do a thing.

And as I watched, in round the Voths gathered shadows. Something was there besides just them. I couldn't
see plain, but I wondered myself were there things like
the Raven Mockers we'd seen and fought and got ourselves away from, back yonder in that open space walled
in by rocks, where was that pool and that dead tree we'd
set afire. I could see Brummitt Voth right well; at least, I
knew him by how tall he was. On his head, instead of his
stylish hat, he wore a sort of cap with points like a rooster
comb, all shiny like some kind of silver. Hooper Voth
showed dumpier in his white rig. I could make out that
he had leaves twisted some sort of fashion round his head
—a wreath, I reckon you call it. Yes, and both had those
ready rifles. One more time, I wished for one of Creed
Forshay's guns, to open up on them with. But all I could
do was take it out in wishing. Which is near about as
much help as an overcoat on a drowning man.

"Get that axe he's carrying," said Brummitt Voth.

Hooper Voth reached out and pulled it away from where it was stuck in Reuben Manco's belt, and held it up in the light for both of them to look at. I saw its blade twinkle.

"I say, you know," said Brummitt Voth, "that's actually what you'd call a tomahawk. When it comes to that, he wears his hair in two long braids. Is this man a red Indian do you suppose?"

"Yuh," said Reuben Manco, deep in his chest. "Me Injun. Yuh."

He'd talked that-a-way at his house, to have fun with Holly Christopher and me, but he wasn't a-funning now. He was a-looking for his own way out of trouble while he played up to them.

"An Indian," Hooper Voth repeated him, and I saw the white of his eye glitter where a moonbeam stabbed down on it. "Are you native to this part of America? Do you live here?"

"Yuh," boomed out Reuben Manco, with those two Voth brothers close on his right and left with their guns, and back in the shadows all those other waiting things, banked up to watch and listen, dark and ugly and on the skulk like the scourings of hell's smokehouse.

"Live here, yuh," he said. "Live along up road yonder, past mountain."

"Oh, ah," said Brummitt Voth, all rough-voiced. "Interesting."

"I begin to see what you mean, Brummitt," said Hooper Voth. "He might be of use to us. Just possibly."

Brummitt Voth put down his face close to Reuben Manco's. "Do you know the beliefs of your Indian tribe?" he asked of him, still mean-sounding. "Do you know what these are here, risen to help us and obey us?"

He took one hand from his gun and waved back to what waited where the shadows were thick. Reuben Manco turned his head, ever so calm and steady, to look all the way behind him. He was a-playing the man, and no I reckon about it.

"Mmmm," he said. "Thinkum maybe-so *anisgina*. Old Cherokee spirit people."

"*Anisgina*," Hooper Voth said the word after him. "Brummitt, I've heard that term somewhere. Possibly I read it in a letter from Jonathan Gibb, years ago. If this Indian happens to have any of the old wisdom, perhaps you're right. He could be a help to us, as you suggest."

"How about that?" Brummitt Voth inquired Reuben Manco above the ready gun. "If we—I say, what's your name?"

"Antoka Manco. White men call me Reuben Manco."

And I'd never before heard his full Cherokee name.

"Very good, Antoka," Brummitt Voth went ahead with him, "if we told you that we are here to bring back the power of your tribe's ancient spirits, would you help us?"

"Me helpum," said Reuben Manco, like as if he was glad to mean it. "Old thing—me knowum old thing, knowum good. Me Cherokee medicine man. Old thing good for Injun."

"Good for all the world," Brummitt Voth said.

Those Voths eased up a bit in the night. What Reuben Manco said to them was a pleasure to hear.

But I, where I listened, figured Reuben Manco to be the liar of the world right then. He was a-playing for time, a-playing like an expert. That meant that he counted on me, for what I could do.

What?

XV

"Now then, let's hold on a minute," said Brummitt Voth. Then he began to talk in the same heap-big-chief way Reuben Manco had been a-giving them.

"You listen good," he said, slow and careful. "Injun medicine heap good, but Druid medicine heap more better. You savvy what I talk?"

"Druid." Reuben Manco brought the word out slow, with those two Voth brothers and their creepy, shadowy followers there to hark at him. "Wagh—what mean Druid?"

"Heap big medicine," Brummitt Voth said, like as if he wanted it to sink in. "Suppose Druid medicine likeum you, it helpum you. Suppose Druid medicine no likeum you, it killum you."

"Wagh," said Reuben Manco, like a man who sees a point made.

Brummit Voth pointed up to where that moon rode high, with clouds near about up to it. "Full moon tonight, you seeum? Druid medicine all-same heap strong this night. Maybe-so Injun helpum, Injun be Druid too. You helpum us, we helpum Injun. Helpum Antoka heap much. Antoka catchum plenty good thing from us, from Druid."

"Yuh," said Reuben Manco. "Me helpum Druid medicine. You tellum how."

"Come along with us, then," Brummitt Voth said. "But you listen good. We watchum you, every move you make.

No foolish business out of you. You catchum what I talk? You savvy?"

"Yuh," said Reuben Manco again. "Me catchum. No fool, me."

It would have been as good as a-being at a play to hear them, if I hadn't been a-wondering the hell out of myself what I must do to give Reuben Manco a saving hand.

"Then you come on," said Brummitt Voth again.

He and his brother started to march Reuben Manco off there along the path among the trees, one of them on each side of him. I saw the drift of the half-shapes of the *anisgina* after them, like a sort of knobby, sooty cloud of smoke. Were they Raven Mockers? If so, such things hadn't been right smart when we'd gone up against them before. We'd been able to get through them then; but with the Voths there, I reckoned they could be dangerous as a hog lot full of rattlesnakes.

I watched them all as they went round a bend. I counted a slow ten to myself, or maybe a twelve, and made myself slip out from my hiding place and follow after them.

If air one of that whole bunch should turn round and look, man or either what wasn't man, I'd been seen, found out, I'd be as good as gone. I came clear from the hemlocks and got into the softer shadows on the path and tippy-toed along to get to some pines farther along. I bent myself down, near about to the ground, so as not to rustle some low-growing needles. I sneaked close up against one pine trunk, on past that to another. I couldn't see right clearly up ahead, but I could hear Hooper Voth's voice, maybe to ask Reuben Manco something or to explain him something.

At least, I figured to myself, the *anisgina* or the Raven Mockers, or whatever the Voths had along with them, couldn't tell them that I'd been out in the night with Reuben Manco. Maybe it would take a Cherokee to talk back and forth to such things. I was glad I was a-being left out of things for the time being, and I made my way along by a-following the sound of the voice.

And, gentlemen, it was no easy job, not by a long shot with a bush in the way. I mustn't let myself be seen or heard or even suspected, that was what I knew right well. So I didn't try to shove myself close behind them. I stayed amongst the thickest trees next the path, I took each step on the heels of my boots to keep from a-making any noise. I bent myself over so low I could near about have crept on my all fours.

At least I knew my way fairly well, this path that led off from the Forshay spring trail up the side of Wolter Mountain to where the Voths lived. Just then, the clouds had drifted themselves more in along the sky, and the moon didn't give all the light it had earlier on. But I was almighty glad of that, because it would make me that much harder to see as I came along. All I had to do was just be double careful, more than double.

Up there ahead, round a bend of the pathway, I could begin to hear them a-talking again. By now they must have about come into the yard of their old stone house, and I'd better watch out how I came into it, too.

So I kept up my sneaky crawl, the way I'd already done; up behind a tree, then a look to see where next; on to maybe a bush, then on beyond to another tree, always a-holding to the very side of the path. In the chunk of sky I saw overhead, clouds had bunched up, as dark and thick as mud. But a hole kept open among them, right at the very top of the sky, a pale, shimmery blaze of light.

One of the Voths, Brummitt as I reckoned, spoke so I could hear his words:

"Just what was it you happened to be doing out on this mountain tonight, Antoka Manco."

"Is heap big medicine night for Cherokee Injun," Reuben Manco replied him back. "All same like heap big night for Druid, what you say. Me come out here all by my lone, pray to old Injun gods."

"And we're doing that same thing tonight," said Hooper Voth. "We're invoking your Indian powers as well as our Druid powers. The two, we dare hope, will work as one. Tell us, have you got any iron on your person?"

"You takeum tomahawk," said Reuben Manco. "Here, got knife. You takeum too."

And Lord have mercy, he was being as smart as smart, every second of the time. When he disarmed his own self that-a-way, he disarmed the Voths.

"Thank you, Antoka," Hooper Voth said, like as if Reuben Manco was the dirt under his feet. "See here then, we'll put your tomahawk and the knife over here to one side, on this stump. Iron doesn't greatly please the old spirits, Antoka. They came to power before the age of iron. Bronze is more pleasant to them."

"And sometimes gold," said Brummitt Voth.

By then I was in sight of them, there in their yard, with the shadowy hunch of their pale stone house and that dark-spreading oak tree beyond them. Brummitt Voth held something in his hand. The best I could make it out, it was that gold-plated sickle I'd seen inside their place.

The shiny moon, always up over things, was like the bright eye of death. Its light made a spark flash on the sickle. Brummitt Voth spoke up, loud and clear, almost like the singing of a song:

"It is the very noon of night, the middlemost night of the summer!"

"Oh yes," sang back his brother, and I could hear from

those other things the sound they made, *oooh oooh*. So they had to be the worst of all the *anisgina* kind, they must be the Raven Mockers.

"It is time, and time enough, and high time, for us to worship as faithfully we must," Brummitt Voth rolled out his words. "Worship is the prayerful shedding of red blood."

"Oh yes."

And *oooh oooh*.

There I was, still free and unseen by them, a-swinging loose in the breeze as you might say. But you'd better believe that my own blood went as cold inside me as the bottom of a river on Christmas night. What had kept me free? My hand came up to the front of my shirt, and I touched what hung there. Holly's elephant charm, the Gilushti figure. Had that kept me safe and hidden so far? I hoped so. It had better be so.

I made yet another sneak more to behind a tree, and from there was where I could make out the house clear, and the Voths and Reuben Manco in the yard of it, with the clutter of shadowy shapes farther off and harder to see, under that wide old oak tree where something lived and hung. I knelt down behind a pile of old fallen-down branches, stacked like for firewood.

The bunch of those Raven Mockers held themselves all pressed up together in an ugly clot round the sprawled-out roots of the oak. They seemed to be a-waiting and a-watching, while the two Voths hunkered down where there was what I made out to be a circle of stones, about as wide as a wagon wheel. I saw a flutter of red light, and I knew that they were a-building them a fire there. They stood up again, a-keeping Reuben Manco betwixt them. They looked like two lost hants in their long white gowns.

"Antoka," said Brummitt Voth to Reuben Manco, "if

you watch what is done here by us, what will happen here, you are a witness. You will be one of us."

"Yuh," said Reuben Manco.

"That is true," put in Hooper Voth. "To see is to believe, to believe is to belong. The setting of the moon will see Antoka Manco welcomed into the brotherhood of our power."

"And you will have the power along with us," Brummitt Voth promised Reuben Manco. "You will have the profit along with us. You will be great along with us. Now, you hear what I talk? You savvy?"

"Yuh," said Reuben Manco, a-standing as quiet as a fence post.

"This night will bring us greatness," said Hooper Voth. "The whole world will know our greatness. The whole world will know and be afraid."

Meanwhile, their fire was a-growing itself up amongst the chunks of wood. It shed its light toward the house. Now I could make out that big old man-shaped cage woven of branches and vines, where it leaned against the end wall. Inside it were lumped two dark shapes. I knew those were Holly and Luke, shut up and held prisoner there, helpless, for whatever was set to happen to them.

And all the time, over us all, the black clouds squirmed and wiggled, like as if they had a sort of life to them, like that other black cloud of things that waited round the roots of the oak. The clouds pushed closer to the blazing moon. But they didn't hide it, not yet.

"If you've got a prayer to say with us, say it now," Brummitt Voth bade Reuben Manco.

"Know Injun song," said Reuben Manco. "Injun medicine song."

"Good. Then sing it."

"Yuh."

Reuben Manco started in to slap his hands together, a slow rhythm like a drumbeat. He sang, and I'd heard the words one time before, from another old Indian:

Wahkonda di diu, wah pah din a ton hie,
Wahkonda di diu, wah pah din a ton hie . . .

Only, that was no Cherokee song. Where I'd heard it was in another part of the country. It comes from the old Ghost Dance days of the Sioux tribe. And the Sioux who sang it told me it means something like this:

> God, a man in need,
> I who sing am that one.

I lay low and harked at Reuben Manco a-singing like that, while his hands slapped for a drum, to ask of help from an Indian god. Not from a Cherokee god—right then, those might be a-harking to other voices. And he asked no bit of help for the Voths, he asked it for himself in that bad fix he was in. I harked, and I wondered myself how I might could go about to do some of the helping he needed.

"Bravo!" cried out both the Brummitts when he finished, and the shapes by the oak moaned *oooh oooh*. Raven Mockers or not, they didn't understand that song, maybe because it wasn't sung in Cherokee. Or if they did sort of guess it, they didn't know what Reuben Manco tried to mean by it just then.

"The time is here, Brummitt," said Hooper Voth.

He put up his face to look at the moon with the clouds strung round it, then he pushed his bare arm out of his gown to see the watch on his wrist.

"Midnight, within a minute or thereabouts," he allowed. "And so says the full moon of midsummer."

I'd made one more careful sneak, while they were all

a-harking at Reuben Manco's song. Now I was up to the backyard of the house, just next to its stony rear corner. I could see that cage thing, made like a big, ugly old man in shape, and Holly and Luke slumped together inside it. They'd be low in their minds. I wondered myself, could I make it along to them and use my knife to cut the lashings and maybe give them a chance to get out and run. I reckoned that if I crawled along to them, they might could see me a-coming, and not know what I was and make a noise about it. And that could well finish us, all three.

I felt for my knife. And, by God, it was gone. It must have shaken out of the sheath somewhere, in what I'd been up to on Wolter Mountain.

Wild inside myself, I wondered what to do. When I took that time to study it, I was too late.

"Bring the captives," said Hooper Voth, in a voice like a captain when he gives an order to soldiers.

At the sound of his word, the bunch of Raven Mockers came a-drifting off from the front of the house, round where I could see them again. And once had already been enough, but I shoved close against that rear corner and stuck out just a little piece of my face, to keep watch with one eye. Lord in heaven, how ugly those things were, with their flapping wing-skins and their stubby legs and their mask faces, as they pushed in round the cage. I watched it stir amongst them like as if life had come into it, and then I watched while it was moved off to the front yard, toward the place where the fire was blazed up. They trundled it along the ground. I reckoned I could see Luke a-standing up inside it, with his arms spread out and his hands grabbed hold of the crossbars of branches, the way a man grabs onto the window bars when he's in the jail house.

Beside the fire, the Voths were like two ghosts in their white rigs. They flung on more wood, more wood. The light of the jumped-up flames grew bright and hot. It beat up to show me a long reach-out branch of the big old oak tree above them. A blob of something moved and hung on it, something too black to catch the light, but awful up there, bigger than a man but not a man, not aught I could say it was. I drew back from the corner, to keep the light from a-showing me where I was.

When I pulled back from the rear of the house, I near about bumped into the open shed behind there. I'd half forgotten about it, but I'd been in that shed the day before, like what seemed years ago now, and I could make out in what of the moon's light soaked down on it. Stone-built like the house, old as old, open toward me, like as if the front of it had gone off to the war or some such thing. And all of a sudden quick, my mind told me what was inside there, inside where I'd been.

It came to me like a message from some kind somebody in heaven. I whupped myself round and strained my eyes to see. I couldn't make out the forge in all those shadows, but I caught a fainty glimmer that must be that silver plowshare the Voths had told me they were at the making of.

"Oh yes, you who hear us!" rose the voice of Hooper Voth, like a trumpet a-being blown to wake the dead. "It shall be as it was, you shall have fresh blood to drink!"

"If I could get out of this thing, there'd be blood all right," I heard Luke Forshay speak up.

"Never heed the voice of the captive," bawled Hooper Voth. "He will be a nourishment, a sweet savor unto you!"

"Oh yes!" came in Brummitt Voth. "Oh verily! And power will be upon us here, to do what we choose in the world—"

Oooh oooh, muttered those other things. But nair sound from Reuben Manco. Nor yet from Holly. Most women, I reckon, would have been a-sobbing and a-carrying on. Not Holly Christopher.

"The true time is now, this instant, and the fire burns and hungers," said Brummitt Voth, and his voice had a greedy sound. "Fetch them close, close."

By that time I'd groped into the shed, my hands a-feeling here and there to find what I wanted.

For the Voths had wanted to make a silver plowshare. Because a plow with iron to it would spoil what they were up to. From off somewhere in the past I recollected what I'd heard from a poem, I don't rightly know where. *Iron, cold iron, shall be master of them all.*

Those old gods the Druids had worshiped, the ones the Voths called on, had turned themselves away from iron—didn't like it, feared it. The Voths had told about that to Reuben Manco. Might could iron be the master, the saving thing?

My reaching hands came up against what I'd sought for, a handle of the plow in there for a pattern. I wished now I'd looked harder at it when I was there in the daytime. I hoped it was just a light plow, not a big old sodbuster like what they used on farms in the lowlands.

I moved in to where I could put both my hands on the plow handles. They felt shackly, half-rotten, but I hoped they'd do what had to be done. I slewed the thing round toward the outside and started to shove it toward where the light of the moon flowed down in the yard.

"Midnight!" yelled out Hooper Voth.

"Midnight!" repeated Brummitt Voth after him. "Speak, Antoka Manco, if you believe."

"Midnight," I could hear Reuben Manco say, more soft in the voice.

I'd wagged and worried the plow outside by that time. Right ahead of me, the ground was bare, no tree roots, no brush, just some tufty grass. And it looked right hard-packed under the blazing moon.

Up over me I heard a soft rumble, like as if it might be thunder. That gave me a sudden hope.

I'd have been able to do better if I'd just had me a yellow mule there to drag the thing for me, but it was up to me to do it all by myself. I hiked the plow handles high and jammed the point of the share into the hard ground. I flung on all my weight, put all the strength I had in my back and arms and shoulders into it, to push it deep down to where the moldboards took hold of the ground. Then I heaved back, and I leaned forward and dug in with my heels and I made that plow cut into the ground to start a furrow.

The old handles bucked and fought in my grip, like as if they'd break off, but I made it move. I jammed it forward a yard or so, another yard, another yard, until I thought I'd just fall down under it.

There came a yell and a crash of thunder, such a noise as you'd hear if they fired off a bunch of cannon. A brighter light than the moon jumped up and danced all over the place.

XVI

I reckon I must have got myself knocked down somehow.
I lay for a second with my head all in a spin and a buzz,
and then I could think again. I got myself up on my
hands and knees beside the plow where it stuck in the
ground, and shook myself hard to get back to where I
might could do something.

But there in front of the house, the fire was a-jumping
and a-snapping, like a million yellow-red flags in a high
wind. It was the big oak tree, slapped over with air
spreading branch of it lighted up, and I told myself that
a thunderbolt must have hit it plumb center.

The stormy sky hollered and split itself with noise.
There were likewise voices, raised high to yell and gab-
ble. As I scrambled up on my shaky feet, I cut my eye to
where the sacrifice fire had been lit. The two Voths
looked to be sprawled out there on the ground in their
white rigs. I couldn't make out where Reuben Manco was
for a moment. Then I saw him, a-standing still as a post.
He might could have been stunned, too, but I somehow
doubted it.

By the light of the burning oak branches, I saw that the
man-shaped cage stood away from the end of the house.
If the Raven Mockers or whatever else they were had
started to fetch it, they were pulled away from it now. I
ran into the open and made for the cage. I grabbed hold

of a big pole that was tied with thick, hard-dried vines. Luke Forshay's pale face slammed close and looked at me through the crisscross of bar pieces.

"Let's get you and Holly out of that," I said, a-wishing again I had my knife. I clamped the pole and dragged my hardest on it. It wouldn't tear free.

"Put your man on this," I wheezed at Luke, and he got both his hands on it, too. He shoved hard. I braced a foot and dragged, and those tough vines popped like pistol shots. I almost fell over backward as the pole came away. Luke bent another pole, and then he had enough of a way to squirm himself out. He reached back in to help Holly. I got up and ran toward where the Voths had gone down.

They lay as limp and flat as two rags. A burning branch, heavy as a house timber, had fallen down on them and blazed as it lay across them.

"Don't expect them to get up, John," said Reuben Manco's voice, as calm as ever.

Nor they wouldn't do that thing, I saw at a glance. I know dead men when I see them. At another glance, I realized something else. The branches of the big fallen-down oak made a fire redder and hotter than a furnace, but deep in amongst them, in the very fiery heart of the business, lay wedged another shape. It didn't move a bit more than the two Voths. It seemed to have arms and legs, and the hair all over it was a-burning like grass.

"Yes," said Reuben Manco, "the Man in the Oak."

Sure enough, there'd been talk about him. About what he really was, how he might could have been that old man by the name of Gibb, changed by death into something nasty and scrambly. Well, the lightning, called up when my iron plow grubbed a furrow in the ground, had done the business for him, too.

A big, cold drop of rain plopped down in my face. Another and another. Up there over us, lightning cracked like a whip in the black clouds.

"My vote is for leaving well enough alone here," Reuben Manco said. "Here come those young people. They seem able to travel. Let's all get away from this place."

I drew a big breath and mopped my face. "It looks like a sort of chancy job, a-working our way down that trail," I said, "but after what we've been through this night, I don't feel much scared off from a try at it."

Reuben Manco started out of the yard. "Come on then," he said.

Luke and Holly didn't much appear like as if they'd heard him, but they came. They walked so close together, Luke's big arm round Holly, that I doubted myself could the raindrops get betwixt them.

The weather was a-coming on harder by then. I turned my back on the burning oak and the bodies of the Voth brothers and the other body, and the Raven Mockers who weren't much for mockery just then. I caught up with Reuben Manco and passed him and searched out our way through the woods. I felt glad for the song of the rain. It was just a natural thing, and natural things are right good at times, even when cold water makes a run down the back of your shirt collar. I strained my eyes in the cloudy night to make out where we must go.

I felt along the bends and wiggles in the trail. It didn't truly seem much of a long time to where we struck the ridge, where all those monkey-faced stones were scattered. I reached there first, then Reuben Manco. We picked our way across the stones, with Holly and Luke catching up behind us. The grass was wet and slippery underfoot when we came to where we must drop to the trail. Reuben Manco and I got ourselves down, then reached up for Luke to lower Holly to us like the precious treasure she'd gotten to be with him. He swung himself after her, and right away quick he had his arm round her waist again.

"Holly," said Luke, barely to be heard. "Holly, you're safe now. Safe, Holly."

Just about then, the rain slackened down to a sort of mist, not too hard to see through.

"Oh, Luke," I heard Holly whisper him back. "Such a night as we've lived through and survived. A night for you and me to remember and talk about all our lives."

"All our lives, Holly," he agreed her. "All our whole long lives."

Reuben Manco turned his grin to me. I could only just see it in that soft darkness. "How wonderful to hear them," he said, so that they wouldn't overhear his words. "It makes the sap rise in an old man just to listen."

I put my own voice up louder. "All right, folks," I said. "Mr. Creed Forshay will be a-waiting all by his lone down yonder in the cabin, and I reckon he'll be right proud and happy to open the door and welcome us home again."

I moved slowly out amongst a spatter of wetness from the leaves to feel with my feet for that narrow dim slope of a trail, the height on one side, the deep drop on the other. Holly and Luke were up behind me, a-leaving Reuben Manco to come after them.

"Can we truly make our way back in this dark night?" Holly wondered us.

"Walk with me," Luke bade her, in his voice still kept soft. "I can get you down safe, Holly. I've often been on this trail by night. I know it well."

So I pulled against the steep bluff to let them move on past me. They felt their way out ahead and downward.

The moon was a-making a little light in the sky again, and I could see that Luke kept his arm close round her waist and that she walked near next to him, her head sort of laid against his broad shoulder.

Reuben Manco caught up with me.

"Now then, Brother John," he said, "who must report what happened to the Voths?"

"Somebody else than me, Chief," I replied him. "So far as I feel concerned, they can stay right there where they are till the somebody else comes along and finds them."

"Very wisely said," he nodded me. "It's been a busy night, hasn't it, John? You and I are tired out, both of us. We'll sleep well. But I want to be up at sunrise tomorrow, to sing a certain song."

"Song?" I said after him like an echo.

"Just a Cherokee medicine song of thanks to the rising sun. The sun is stronger than the moon. My song will be to wipe out whatever is left of bad medicine on Wolter Mountain."

"Brother," I said, calling Reuben Manco that for the first time, "I want to get up when you do."

Our hands came together and shook one another.

"I'll be proud to hear you sing that song," I said. "If I knew it, I'd sing it along with you."

"I'll teach it to you, my brother," he made me a promise.